I0554060

Younger & Wylder

by

Shelley White

The Wylder West

This is a work of fiction. Names, characters, places, and incidents are either the product of the author's imagination or are used fictitiously, and any resemblance to actual persons living or dead, business establishments, events, or locales, is entirely coincidental.

Younger & Wylder

COPYRIGHT © 2022 by Shelley E. White

All rights reserved. No part of this book may be used or reproduced in any manner whatsoever without written permission of the author or The Wild Rose Press, Inc. except in the case of brief quotations embodied in critical articles or reviews.
Contact Information: info@thewildrosepress.com

Cover Art by *Diana Carlile*

The Wild Rose Press, Inc.
PO Box 708
Adams Basin, NY 14410-0708
Visit us at www.thewildrosepress.com

Publishing History
First Edition, 2022
Trade Paperback ISBN 978-1-5092-4154-5
Digital ISBN 978-1-5092-4155-2

The Wylder West
Published in the United States of America

"Why'd you marry me then, if you didn't want a wife?"

Race sighed. "I didn't want to see you misused. You reminded me of my—" But she didn't really remind him of Mary Catherine at all. Technically, he was old enough to have fathered her. His stomach turned, renewing the nausea he'd been battling all morning. "You remind me of my friend's little sister. I didn't like the look of Mr. Monroe. Not that you were given a choice, but it was him or me."

She thought on this for a moment, then said, "I thank you, I s'pose, but I don't know you either. If I'm not to act like your wife, what am I supposed to do?"

"Think of me as a wise older brother."

"Wiser than who? You'd better not say me. You're the one saddled with a wife you don't want."

She wasn't wrong in her assessment. "How about just an older brother, then?"

She eyed him up and down. "So's I can marry someone else someday when boys come a courtin'?"

Regret filled him. He'd trapped them both in his hasty rescue. "We're still a few years off from worrying about that. We'll ford that river when we get to it."

Millie slumped in her seat. "I'm sorry for ruining yer life."

"It was already ruined and, on its way, to getting worse. You most likely saved my life and gave me something to live for, the next few years. Maybe by the time you're grown, I'll have figured out what to do with the rest of it."

Other Wild Rose Press Titles by Shelley White

Ginger Snapped
Penny Gothic: a romance of fictitious proportions
Square Penny: Romance and Mystery Afoot

Dedication

To John, always.
Special thanks to Ally, Kim, & Nicole.

Prologue

Scotts Bluff, Nebraska Territory, 1848

Horace 'Race' Lowery leaned back in his chair, surveying the pile of coins in front of him. The deed to a mercantile in Santa Fe was the latest addition to his winnings courtesy of the player across the table. This game was the latest detour on his path to destruction. Lady Luck had fastened herself around his neck like an anchor and he'd become relatively wealthy for a man who didn't care if he lived or died. Even somewhat intoxicated, he knew his luck would eventually run out, and he'd be able to get on with the business of being miserable.

Eventually came when Millie Spooner stepped into the room.

Otis had been crowing about his virgin daughter all night and hinting at the outdated notion of a bride price. Race got the impression the man was out to sell his daughter but only half-listened and missed the details. He wasn't in the market for another wife. No one deserved to be subjected to his misery, let alone a woman. But Millie wasn't a woman.

Race checked into his room at the Spooner Boarding House in Scotts Bluff, earlier in the afternoon. The owner, Otis, took one look at his gold pocket watch and invited him to play a couple hands at that evening's parlor card game. After ensuring whiskey would be cheap and plentiful, he agreed to stop by.

He stowed his catalog case and saddle bags and refilled his flask from his personal bottle of high-end No. 9, just in case he couldn't stomach Spooner's swill. Before heading to the game, he unwrapped the double photo frame from the cloth that protected it. His vibrant Rosemary and fair Mary Catherine stared up him. Race thought life unfair when, at sixteen, he lost his mother in the 1832 cholera epidemic. He was reminded how cruel life could be when his wife and daughter succumbed to the same disease eight months ago. He was grateful to his employer and friend for allowing him to take over travel sales when he couldn't bear his empty house anymore.

Race drew his thoughts back to the situation before him. Beneath hooded eyes, he took the measure of his fellow players. The railroad man that used to own the mercantile wore a look of confusion and disgust. The man next to Otis never took his eyes off his cards. The player to Race's left leered at Otis's daughter. He snaked his hand to his lap and rubbed at his groin.

Millie placed a steaming bowl in front of each man, moving in and out of each players' personal space, somehow not brushing or bumping any of the men. The man next to Race shifted, causing his shoulder to graze her breast. She jumped back, then caught herself and mumbled, "S'cuse me." Her eyes darted between each man, growing wider as she moved around the table. Her hand trembled as she set the last bowl in front of her father.

"Thank you, Millie darlin'. Those beans look right tasty. You go on to bed now." Otis smacked his daughter on the bottom as she left the room. The door swung shut on her panicked backward glance. Otis turned back to the group at the table. "What did I tell ya? Pretty as a picture, isn't she?"

The railroad man set his cards on the table. "How old is she, man? She's not but a child."

"Old enough to be wed and bed. She's fourteen, but she's a woman a'ficially. Are you ready to talk bride price?"

"I should say not. I don't want any part of this." He picked up the few coins remaining in front of him and dropped them in his pocket before stalking out the door.

"What about the rest of yous?"

Race sobered. Fourteen years old. His own daughter had been eight, and he wouldn't have ever willingly parted with her, let alone use her as a commodity. What kind of man did that? He'd give anything—anything—to have his daughter back in his arms. He'd protect her with his life. Otis's booze was midgrade, but at this point churned and threatened to resurface. He should leave, but he'd latched on to the idea of protecting the girl from her own father. He just didn't know how yet. He looked around the table at the two men who stayed. One appeared ready to bolt. He eyed the pot with a longing that kept him glued to his seat.

The man seated beside Race claimed a pile nearly as big as his own. Otis called him Monroe, but it was unclear whether it was a first or last name. His accent placed him from the South, as did his shiny shoes and black brocade jacket, both out of place in this neck of the woods. He played well, reminding Race of professional gamblers in bigger cities. Millie's appearance didn't seem to disturb him. His earlier leer had been replaced with an innocent, besotted expression. One Race didn't believe for a second.

"What kind of bride price are ya thinkin' about?" Monroe pulled a tobacco twist out of his pocket and bit off the end. He used his tongue to lodge it between his jaw and cheek pouch.

Otis went behind the bar and came back with a charcoal stub and scrap of paper. He wrote down a figure and slid it across the table.

Monroe flipped it over and considered it while moving the tobacco to the other cheek with his tongue. "Hmm. Too rich for my blood, I think. Why don't we play a few more rounds, see if I can't improve my lot."

Race met Otis's hopeful stare but made no response. Otis sighed and dealt the next round.

As the night wore on, the whiskey flowed. Race pretended inattention and paced himself. He refilled often to give the appearance of overindulgence without ever taking more than a few sips out of each full glass. He had a bad feeling about how the night was proceeding. Otis matched the much larger Monroe drink for drink. Though Millie didn't make another appearance, her image was burned on Race's brain like a nightmare.

Millie looked nothing like Mary Catherine. His daughter had been angelic, blonde and frail with the prettiest blue eyes. She couldn't stay in the sun but a minute or she'd turn red as a berry. Not only was Millie older, but also darker complected with curling brown hair and gray eyes. She was sturdier, too. Not quite plump, but Millie looked healthier than Mary Catherine did, even before she got sick.

4

No, the comparison Race couldn't shake was that of a girl wearing a dress sizes too big and playing with her mamma's toilette. Mary Catherine invited him to tea once wearing one of Rosemary's old dresses. She'd used Rosemary's scented talc to powder her face. She smelled like roses and looked like a ghost, but he didn't laugh at his little girl trying to look grown up.

Millie's dress fit everywhere but the bust, which was lumpy and lopsided. Her curls, which had been secured with combs at some point earlier in the day, protested their confinement and had either escaped or gone frizzy. The face paint was the worst of it. Red covered her lips and circled her mouth obscenely. The rouge on her cheeks and eye powder brought to mind the war paint on a dead Indian Race saw in Illinois.

A look that had been sweet and endearing on Mary Catherine made Millie look like a cheap whore. Race wanted to vomit. None of this was his concern, but he couldn't bring himself to leave the table. So, he played and drank and watched his host get drunker and drunker.

Monroe appeared to plan his wins and losses as best he could in a game of chance. Every time Otis's drink was empty, he refilled it, while never quite emptying his own. One of the lanterns went out, but no one bothered to relight it. The odor of Otis's alcohol tainted sweat hung over the table like a cloud. Race wished he had a cigar to light to cut through it though it likely would have turned into a ball of fire from the alcohol fumes.

Monroe folded his hand and tossed his cards. "I just don't know if tonight is my night, Otis. I would surely love to take your beautiful daughter home as my wife, but I didn't bring quite enough money with me on this trip, and I seem to be doing a piss poor job of winning any tonight."

Listing to the right, Otis puffed up his chest. "W-well, I stand firm on my, on my offer. She's worth all that an' more. She's been keepin' house here for near bout eight years."

"Oh, I can tell she's special. I'm half in love with her already. I guess it just wasn't meant to be. I think I'm gonna turn in. I sure wish there was another way." Monroe pulled his hat off the back of his chair and placed it on his head. Then his eyes lit up. "Hey, here's an idea. Maybe I could win her hand."

"Win her hand?" Otis stared at him blankly.

Monroe acted as if he was warming up to this new idea. "Yes, yes. Like the knights of old that would compete for the hand of a fair maiden."

"Millie?"

"Millie's as fair a maiden as I've ever seen. How about I compete for her hand right here."

"What?" Not clever to begin with, Otis proved even more malleable with drink.

Monroe removed his hat. "One more hand. For Millie. Let me earn her, Otis. Prove to you I'm a winner."

"I'm out." The gambler across the table scooped his meager winnings into his own hat and high-tailed it out the door.

Otis eyed Monroe's modest pile. Race could almost see the alcohol-laced calculations trying to happen in Otis's head. The man didn't seem to understand that if Monroe won, Millie would be his free and clear. Race would not coach the man on how to sell his daughter.

Otis's eyes flicked to Race and his bigger pile of coins. "What about you?"

Leave. Walk away.

He glanced at Monroe and choked back his gorge rising at the thought of the man putting his hands on the young girl. He'd run across men like Monroe in the past. No father worth his salt would let a man like that within ten feet of his child.

"I'm in."

Chapter 1

Nebraska Territory, 1854

Millie glanced at her husband from behind her bonnet. Race's tired eyes squinted at the horizon. Endless miles of prairie lay ahead but not as many as lay behind. A gentle breeze rippled through the new spring grasses, bringing relief from the midday sun. She loved this time of year. No matter the past, there was always a chance for a new beginning.

Race blinked, and Millie averted her gaze. He pulled the horses to a halt and turned to her.

"Are you sure you want to stop in Scotts Bluff? I'd hoped to avoid it. We need to split off this route soon if you want to skirt around it. We'll need to ration our supplies a little tighter." Race removed his hat and combed his hair back from his face. He pulled the hat back to secure it, but a few black locks escaped near his temple. Creases bracketed his brown eyes, a result of many days spent traveling. Millie's youth and wide brim protected her from a similar fate but not from a freckled nose.

"You couldn't have predicted Indian trouble along the direct route. We're lucky we got word in enough time to avoid it. Besides, I want to see Bethesda. We weren't in Iowa City long enough for her letters to catch up with me. I don't want to risk the next leg without replenishing supplies. I'll be fine." She put a tentative hand on his knee. It fell away when he faced forward and flicked the reins.

"I know you'll be fine. You're strong. I don't want you to have to see your father. *I* don't want to see your father. I should have laid him out six years ago." He scowled at the emptiness ahead of them.

She folded her hands in her lap to avoid further rejection. "He can't hurt me anymore." She changed the subject. "Do you think they have Indian trouble in Wylder?" She'd heard terrible stories, but never encountered any natives herself.

"I don't know. They've got a bank, so they must have a big enough population to support it. Maybe they trade with the nearby tribes in a mutually beneficial arrangement. If you don't treat 'em fairly, it generally doesn't go well for the white man; or the Indians in the end."

The Millie traveling back to the place of her birth was no longer the naïve girl with firm ideas on how the adults in her life should behave. As an adult, she understood sometimes life gave you frustrations but not the skills to handle them. She glanced again at her husband, currently her chief frustration. She shifted in her seat and sighed, arching her aching back and jiggling her left foot which was going numb.

"I'm sorry we weren't in Iowa City very long. I've got enough set back now, maybe we can buy a place in Wylder and settle for a while. I'll do the clock installation the bank ordered and see if we like the town. Sound good?"

"Sure." She met Race's gaze. "Maybe it will be a good place to start a family."

Soon they'd be starting over in a new town, a new territory, and she planned to start fulfilling her status in a new way. When they arrived in Wylder, she'd be sure to be introduced as Race's wife for the first time. She wasn't his sister, and it was time he realized that. How to make it happen had her stumped.

He winced. "I'll look into retaining a lawyer who can help us with a quiet annulment. But you don't need to go rushing out to find a beau. Let's settle into town first, get to know people."

Millie smirked. She wouldn't let Race play dumb anymore when she made references to their future. He loved her, like kin, at least. She needed to figure out how to push him over that last step.

Her heart had been his before they'd even reached Santa Fe six years ago. He'd been so kind and respectful, like nothing she'd ever experienced. He never assumed she'd do all the cookin' and washin'. He asked her opinion and explained his decisions. He'd treated her like his favorite sister. For the past. Six. Years.

She'd seen so much and grown so much since then—mountains bigger than she could've imagined, steam locomotives, people of all colors. In her birth territory alone there'd been tallgrass prairies as far as the eye can see and new baby orchards cropping up along their journey. Her new skills included running a mercantile. She could measure out everything from fabric to dry goods, and even turned a respectable hand to sewing new clothes for herself and Race.

She learned how to be a helpmate to Race in almost all ways. When he succumbed to bouts of melancholia, she knew when to leave him be and when to draw him out. He shared with her about his poor wife and daughter and how much he still missed them, and she told him what her mother had written in the letters Bethesda gave her.

Race learned about her too. With no one to rely on but each other, his brotherly concern helped ease her embarrassment over womanly issues that came up over the years. Race knew she understood why her mother left but wasn't ready to forgive. And that Millie's younger sister, Winnifred, lived with the mother Millie hadn't seen since she was four.

"We have another two nights of sleeping rough before we get to Scotts Bluff," Race said, interrupting her thoughts.

"Will we get one room or two when we get there? Everyone there knows we're married."

Race's jaw was doing the ticking thing more often the closer they got to Scotts Bluff. "Two. I don't much care what people know or what Otis thinks."

"Well, I do! Everyone will think I'm a bad wife and you put me out." She honestly didn't care what anyone thought either. She could explain things to Bethy. But this seemed like the time to start her campaign for being a real wife. Too bad Race was having none of it.

"Sorry, Millie. I know we usually talk things through, but I'm firm on this."

"You just don't want to sleep with me," she accused, folding her arms in a huff.

More ticking and a sigh from Race. "We'll talk about it later."

Millie snorted. As if they didn't have all the time in the world for the next two days to talk.

****

1848

What the hell was he going to do with the girl? Otis expected him to marry Millie this morning. When Race explained that by winning the game, he didn't have to pay the bride price, his host was irate. Monroe stepped in and offered to pay for the privilege, but Race shoved a pile of money in Otis's direction, ending the discussion.

Without the benefit of marriage, Millie was still Otis's property. Race couldn't take her with him or protect her if he left. He wouldn't leave her to Monroe or an even worse fate. He picked up the images of his wife and child, wrapped them, and stowed them away. He donned his cleanest set of clothes and laced up his boots. He never planned to have another wedding day. The horror of his impending nuptials caused bile to churn in his gut. Breakfast was out of the question.

He checked in on his horse, Del, at the livery and inquired about purchasing a small wagon and second horse. The stable master could handle both requests, so Race asked him to have everything hooked up and ready for him at noon.

He stopped in at the mercantile, his original purpose for visiting Scotts Bluff, gave a half-hearted spiel on the virtues of E. Howe clocks, then picked out all the things he hadn't needed when traveling alone.

"I don't have a need to carry clocks regular, but if I can keep this catalog, I can show it to folks who ask," the shop owner said.

"That's fine. It's what it's for. There's information on the back on how to place an order." He set the last items he picked out on the counter. "I'm ready, this'll

be all."

"Hear you're marrying the Spooner girl. Might young, Millie is." The man's voice was laced with censure.

"I am, and she is." He hated small towns with nosey people. He warred with the need to defend himself, to tell the man that Otis essentially sold her. In the end, he simply stated, "I'm better than the alternative."

"Mmm. I imagine that's probably so." The man totaled up Race's purchases. "Come by on your way out of town this afternoon. I'll have the missus pack you something for the trip."

Race didn't know how the man knew when he was leaving town since he'd only just made the arrangements, but he welcomed free food in any form. At least he seemed to understand the situation enough not to judge him too harshly. He nodded. "Much obliged."

"She's a nice girl. Don't deserve her lot."

Race nodded. He couldn't agree more.

****

Millie was going to be the death of him. If the calvary ever needed a suggestion on how to torture a man, Race would put up Millie's curvy little body. For the past two years, looking at her like a sister had become a challenge, and every day it got worse.

She'd never been too young for him by the world's standards, only his own. The age gap still existed, but now, even by his standards, she was old enough to be married. But not to him. She deserved better than a broken-down widower who couldn't get over losing his first family. Though, lately, Race began to wonder if he was clinging to Rosemary's memory because he truly missed her, or out of habit, to avoid his growing awareness of his wife.

He loved her. He cared for her all this time as a brother and friend. The possibility of changing status made him uncomfortable. On a day-to-day basis, it was easy to see her as Millie, his friend and sister. The problem arose when she caught him unawares. For instance, in the morning when they met in the kitchen and her hair hung all wavy down her back. Once, she made herself a new dress. Race caught himself admiring the shape of a woman shopping in the mercantile. It wasn't till she turned he realized it was Millie. When she fell asleep in her chair by the fire, she didn't look childlike anymore. Relaxed and seductive, it wasn't difficult to picture her that way in his bed.

He'd taken to walking out his frustration, usually winding up at either the Episcopalian or Catholic churches in town. Neither faith fit right anymore and rightly so. His conversion to Catholicism was superficial at best and blasphemous at worst. As a result, he didn't feel welcome in either the faith of his calling nor the faith of his wife and daughter. He'd given up a candidacy in the former after meeting the love of his life. He resented the latter for not providing him with what he needed to heal in his time of greatest need. Upon reflection, he was at fault for not committing fully to the faith.

Yet, he still sought solace in both pews. He sought direction from the protestant faith and went to the Catholics to confess his growing confusion about his legal wife. He never actually entered a confessional. How would he ask forgiveness for having carnal thoughts about his own wife? The priest would kick him out and send him forth to multiply. No, his confessions were between him and the Lord, but there were no answers there either.

The miles of prairie dragged on. His skin tingled whenever Millie studied him. His body would start itching like he had hives. The early May sun, though kind in the mornings, made him sticky and even more uncomfortable in the afternoons. Millie wore her bonnet so he couldn't see her face, but the tingles always gave her away.

"I see it!" She stood and clamped a hand onto his shoulder to steady herself in the bumpy wagon. "I see the bluffs! We'll be there before dinner. Lord, I need a real bath." She laughed and plopped herself in the seat, her thigh pressed into his.

Race shifted away and studied the bluffs as they came into view. Anything to take away the image of Millie bathing.

"Are you ready to talk about sharing a room?" She met his gaze with intent.

"Nothing to talk about. We're leaving early tomorrow, and I need my rest. I'll either rent a second room for you or you can stay in your old room in Otis's apartment. You can tell folks it's so you don't wake me when you come to bed after visiting if you like." That sounded plausible to his mind.

"We've been married six years. Folks'll wonder why we don't have young'uns."

"Tell 'em you're barren," Race snapped.

Millie sucked in her breath. "Race! I will not."

Bad form. "I'm sorry, Mills, I shouldn't have said that. I'm tired. Tell 'em I'm barren."

Millie burst into laughter. His jest covered his insensitive words and distracted her from the previous line of questioning.

****

"Yer back. Six years of nothin' and now you expect me to put ya up?" Otis had put on some girth since Millie'd been gone. Surprising, as he'd have been seeing to his own meals.

Bethesda smacked him on the arm. "Stop it, Otis. I've told you all about how the girl's been every time I got a letter." She pulled Millie into a welcoming hug. "Darlin, I'm so glad you're home."

"It's just a quick stop," Race cut in. "We're leaving tomorrow for Wylder. You don't need to put anyone up, Otis. I'll pay for rooms."

Millie hooked her arm with Bethesda's before anyone could comment on the rooms, plural. "Bethy, I would give my left leg for a hot bath. Can I use your room so we can visit while I bathe?" She led the woman toward the stairs that led to her rooms, leaving Race to answer uncomfortable questions.

"How many rooms you want?" Otis asked. He spit chewing tobacco on the ground near his feet.

"Two."

"She high-falutin like her momma? I ain't takin her back. Used goods an too, set in 'er ways by now."

Race resisted the urge to punch the despicable man. "You can't have her back. Do you have two rooms available or not? I don't have any problem continuing on tonight after the horses have rested."

"Nah, yer money's as good as anyone else's. Probably better." He cackled and tobacco juice dribbled down his chin; it must be a new habit. "Still playin' poker in the parlor. You in?"

Race was tempted to clean the man out. On the rare occasion he took in a game, he still found himself to be uncommonly lucky. Card playing led to drinking and that often led to bad decisions. With Millie close at hand and hell bent on driving him crazy, he'd best keep his wits about him. "Last time I played with you, I took your daughter. You better ask yourself what else you think you can stand to lose before you invite me to play again. Why don't you just show me what rooms we can use and decide whether or not you're going to treat your daughter like family or a commodity. Then you can stay the hell out of my way." Race picked up Millie's bag and started up the stairs, leaving Otis sputtering behind him.

****

1848

Bethesda helped Millie into her nicest dress. "I got a look at him. If there's one thing I can do, it's read men. This is not an ideal situation, darlin', but between the two fellas out there, you got the better deal."

Millie pulled at the hair wisping around her temples and Bethesda slapped her hand away. "Why's he in such a hurry? We ain't even been properly introduced an he's ready to quit town."

The older woman unwrapped the twine from Millie's hair and started untwisting the braids. "Hear me out. Race Lowery is a broken-down man. You got a fifty-fifty chance he'll turn that brokenness on you. That happens, you lay low when you sense a mood coming on. But I don't get that feel about him." She began brushing Millie's hair out from crown to tip. "Now the other fella, Tipton Monroe, he can't hide a thing from

17

me with that poker face of his. With him you'd have a hundred percent chance of being mistreated. His kind are cruel and like it rough." She finished by twisting the hair up into a bun and securing it with four pins.

Millie turned and hugged the woman who'd mothered her for the past ten years. "I'm glad you're here. I wish you were my momma."

Bethesda sat back and looked Millie in the eyes. "I've explained why your momma couldn't stay. Otis may be a useless daddy, but he was a far worse husband. He was jealous and spiteful and broke your momma's spirit. I won't get into the details; they ain't important for you to know. But when the chance came, I encouraged her to go and promised to look after you." She cocked her ear toward the door. "I hear your daddy bellowing. It's time to go."

Chapter 2

After six more days on the road, Millie was more than ready for the journey to be over. They slept rough, only getting to enjoy a bed in Bear Springs and Cheyenne City. Race said they'd be in Wylder before dark. After a month of grassy plains, it excited her to see hills in the distance.

Millie touched Race's arm. 'More touching' was the first step in her plan to gain his notice. She didn't have any other steps thought out yet. "Race, what's that ahead of us?" They watched the road dust billow and churn until the shape of a coach could be discerned.

"Stage. They travel fast. I usually try to avoid stage lines for that reason. Find something to cover your face before it gets here." He pulled a bandana out of his pocket and handed Millie the reins while he tied it in place.

When the coach drew closer, Race pulled as far to the right as he could without getting stuck. The driver didn't even look their way as he barreled past. When the dust settled, they got their first glimpse of their new home, Wylder.

Millie's excitement built as the town grew larger before them. Her real married life would start here. She'd get Race to realize she wasn't a little girl anymore and they'd start a family. She pulled a small daguerreotype out of her pocket and rubbed her thumb over the image. She didn't even look like the girl in the picture anymore, let alone act like her. She'd worked hard to fit into Race's world. Her speech was better, more like Race's polished, east-coast accent. She'd gotten better at taming her unruly curls and her clothes rivaled those of a banker's wife.

Yes, Wylder was her chance at a new beginning.

****

1848

She tried to focus on Preacher Dan's words. Her thoughts swirled in her head and kept distracting her. "What? Yer name's Horace?" She stifled a snort.

Race's jaw ticked. "My Christian name is Horace Charles, but I go by Race for obvious reasons."

"Horace and Mildred. We sound old, like people in their fifties." She smiled, then froze. "Oh! You're not in your fifties are you? I didn't mean no offense."

Race's jaw ticked again. "I'm thirty-three. Race and Millie will suit for now. Can we continue, please?"

"Oh. Sorry. Yes, please continue."

The rest of the short service concluded quickly. Millie relaxed slightly until she heard the pastor say, "You may kiss the bride." Her breath caught in her throat, and she couldn't move. She envisioned Race's bristled face closing in on her.

"Come on, Millie. Time to go." Race tugged at her hand, pulling her with him up the aisle.

She didn't know whether to be relieved of disappointed that he didn't kiss her. They stepped outside and she saw a wagon parked next to her father's. A small table with a black box on it sat in the middle of the churchyard.

"Miss Millie." A tall thin man approached

wringing his hat in his hands. "Miss Bethesda hired me to make your wedding daguerreotype."

"Oh." Millie pulled at Race's hand. "Race, can we? Bethy went to the trouble to get Leonard here."

Race stood next to her in front of the church while Leonard fiddled with the black box. Race reminded her of a coyote tensed to nab a jackrabbit. He barely stilled for the few moments it took to make the image. As soon as Leonard said he'd finished, Race released her hand and went to transfer her small trunk out of her father's wagon.

Her father, Mr. Monroe, and Bethesda came out of the church. Bethesda drew her into a tight hug and whispered in her ear. "You write and tell how you're gettin' on, all right?" Millie nodded. "I put a packet of letters from your momma in the bottom of your trunk. You read 'em. They'll help you understand. Love you, darlin.'"

Bethy stepped away and her father stepped in and hugged her briefly. "You'll be fine."

Millie sniffed and wiped away tears. "Love you, Papa."

****

Race approached Wylder with the same trepidation he did when they moved to other new towns. Being responsible for another besides himself weighed on him. When he used to travel alone, he never worried about sleeping rough or scanty meals. Back then he would have welcomed bandits to kill him and put him out of his misery.

He had to commend Millie, though. She never complained, and she did all she could to lessen his physical load, if not his mental. He tried to hide his worries from her.

His friend and boss, Gunther Stephens, at E. Howe Clock Co. had written him of a bank in Wylder that needed help installing the clock they'd ordered. Race exchanged letters with Alfred Mountroy, the owner, who assured him Wylder was an up-and-coming town, soon to rival Cheyenne. From what Race could see so far, Mountroy was either disillusioned or optimistic.

Millie gripped Race's arm. "Race, Indians!"

How she could tell the two people leading a horse were Indians from such a distance, he had no idea. "Your eyes must be better than mine. How can you tell?"

"Their clothing and hair. Aren't you concerned?"

"They hardly look like they're on the warpath." As they drew nearer, Race could see the men were Indians and their horse, loaded down with skins, wasn't racing off to fight anytime soon. They were heading toward town but staying off the main road. For good reason, many would shoot first and ask questions later. "They look like they're coming to town to trade. Not all tribes are violent."

Millie relaxed and loosened her grip on his arm but didn't release him. "Do you think Wylder has any trouble with Indians?"

"From what Mr. Mountroy said in his letter, Wylder is on its way to becoming an advanced little metropolis. I have my doubts, but if they have a bank with a clock, they can't be too uncivilized," Race reasoned.

"And there'll be a place for your clock shop?" Millie moved her hand to his thigh.

He nodded "Your dress shop, too. Mr. Mountroy

says there are a couple locations that would work." He tried to ignore the tingling her hands set off in his leg. *Sister, sister, sister* he chanted to himself.

"I don't know, Race. I've only ever sewn clothes for us. I don't know if I'm good enough to hang out a shingle."

"Mountroy said the town doesn't have any, how'd he put it, feminine-type shops as of yet. If you simply call yourself a seamstress, you'll probably get plenty of business mending garments for miners and cowboys."

Millie wrinkled her nose. "I don't want to spend all day mending dirty mining clothes. Are there even any women living there? Why are they so hard-up for women's stores?"

Race shifted in his seat, hoping to escape Millie's hand. "I'm sure there are. Can't have a town full of men with no women."

She snorted and moved her hand to her lap. "I meant respectable women. I'm sure there are the other kind who make their money off towns full of men."

Race blushed. "I'm sure there are lots of wives, too."

Millie bounced in her seat again. "Look, a little steeple! I wonder what kind of church it is."

Race noted that Millie's excitement over the church was on his behalf. They never attended services, but he frequented the building often enough. Never found the answers he sought, but he kept coming back, seeking them.

The first town building they came to was nothing more than a big, dusty barn. If the horses in the attached corral didn't identify the building, the cart parked next to it full of manure surely did. "There's the livery.

Mountroy said we should leave our wagon here and the bank was just a short walk." He pulled around the corral and parked in front. A lean-to jutted out from the side of the livery, providing cover for a small blacksmith forge.

A man a little younger than Race came out to greet them. "Welcome to Wylder. You looking to board or passing through? I'm Chet Daniels." He shook hands with Race.

"Board. We have business at the bank before it closes. We'll come back for our bags. What time do you close?" Race reached up to help Millie down.

"Live on the premises. If'n I'm not around front, feel free to come around the side and knock." Chet stepped away from the couple and yelled into the building. "Jackson! You got those stalls mucked?"

A tall, rangy youth came around the corner. "All ready, Pop."

"Come pull this wagon in and unhitch it." Chet turned to Race. "Jackson'll stay out until you all return."

Race acknowledged the youth as he passed and nodded his thanks. To Chet he said, "Much obliged. Can you point the way to the bank?"

"And tell us what kind of church that is." Millie interrupted, pointing to the wooden, steepled structure across from the livery.

"That there is the Episcy-palian church. You'll pass the Papist building on the way to the bank." Chet pointed northwest. "Quickest way is to cut through behind the land office. The other church will be on your left and the very next building is the bank."

Race ignored the derogatory remark. Once upon a

time he would have referred to Catholics similarly. He thanked the man again and led Millie in that direction. They passed the church, small compared to the Episcopalian's, then came to a half-finished sandstone foundation. They emerged onto a busier street. Race noted a law office on his right. The unfinished structure must be the bank. That couldn't be right.

They turned left and found, next to the construction, a modest wooden building with a sign that read Goldmount Bank Alfred Mountroy, Owner. "This is it." He guided Millie inside. She'd been quiet thus far, taking in her new surroundings.

Goldmount Bank was not what he expected. How in the world did Mountroy intend to mount the heavy clock on this ramshackle wooden building? Race guessed he'd find out soon enough.

Chapter 3

The inside of the bank was as primitive as the front façade. Millie hoped they'd finish the new building before the walls of the old one fell down around them. She could see tendrils of sunlight filtering through some of the wall panels.

"Can I help you?" A balding man in his fifties wearing a fancy gray suit stood up from behind a desk.

"I'm Horace Lowery. I'm from E. Howe Clock Company to help you with your clock."

The man brightened. "Mr. Lowery, I'm so glad you're here. I can't wait to show her to you. She's a fine specimen." He took Race's hand and nearly shook it off his arm with enthusiasm. "I'm Alfred Mountroy. Please, call me Alfred."

Race forcibly extracted his hand and smiled at the man. "And you can call me Race. This is my—"

"I'm Mildred Lowery, Race's wife." Millie shot forward and offered her hand to the banker, ignoring Race's horrified expression.

"Er, um, it's a pleasure, ma'am. I wasn't aware Mr. Lowery was bringing a wife. I thought he mentioned a sister?" He shook her hand with far less exuberance, barely grasping her fingertips.

"An oversight, I'm sure," she demurred. "His sister bowed out of the trip at the last minute."

Race clenched his jaw and his eye ticked. "Yes. An

oversight. A grave miscalculation." He spoke to Mountroy but glared at Millie.

"Yes, well. No harm done. Would you like to see my clock?" He bounced a little on his heels.

"Actually, we've traveled quite a piece today. I'm anxious to see your clock and your plans, but right now, I'd really like to get my s—wife settled. Can you spare a moment to point us to a hotel or boarding house?"

"Oh! Of course. My apologies. I'll take you myself." He poked his head into a doorway behind him. "Fredrick, come out and meet the man who's going to install our clock."

A young man of no more than eighteen emerged from the back room. He, too, was wearing a finely tailored suit, or it had been. His tall frame, broad shoulders, and narrow waist caused the coat to strain across his upper back and his sleeves fell about two inches too short. His slacks fit no better. He appeared to be the victim of a recent growth spurt.

"This is my son, Fredrick. One day this will all be his." The banker waved his arm at the space that barely looked sturdy enough to stand, let alone store money. He must have noticed his guests' skeptical looks. "Well, not this. We're rebuilding next door. Something with more permanence. That's where the clock will go. Fredrick, this is Mr. and Mrs. Lowery."

Race's teeth ground together as he shook the young man's hand. "A pleasure,' he said.

"Fred, I'm going to lock you in while I take the Lowerys on a brief tour. It's close enough to closing time; you can go ahead and start on closing procedures." He pulled a large ring of keys from his pocket.

Fredrick looked annoyed for a moment, then smoothed his features. "Yes, Sir."

"Come along, then." Alfred led them out of the building, and after locking up, turned to the new construction. "You see we have the foundation laid, but work is a bit stalled at the moment. I wanted to make the whole thing out of stone. I said, 'If it's good enough to hold munitions at Ft. Laramie, then why shouldn't we use it to protect Wylder's money?' Alas, not all of the investors have the vision required to be willing to fund such an endeavor."

"The building won't all be stone? I'm not sure how we're going to mount the clock you purchased." Race scratched his chin through his thick beard.

"I ordered the clock when I thought we'd be able to build with stone. It's the same model as in St. Louis. Did you know that? Beautiful piece." The man gazed at the foundation as if envisioning the finished construct.

"Do you know where you'd like to place it?" Race persisted.

"I'd like it mounted outside, right near the entrance. Nothing says 'established' like an outside street clock, I say. Well, come along. Let's get you situated before it gets dark."

Millie shielded her eyes against the setting sun. Alfred pointed out landmarks along the way. The town wasn't difficult to figure out. "This is why my building is still unfinished." A much larger building was going up on the other side of the old bank. "This will be the Vincent House Hotel and Restaurant. Granted, I begrudge them stealing my work crew, but the Vincent will rival the nicest establishments in Cheyenne when it's finished. I look forward to having someplace in town worthy of treating my wealthy clients.

"The sheriff's office and jail are across the street. Handy for the bank, though we don't see too much trouble. This is the more civilized side of town."

Millie wondered what the man considered too much trouble. The street they were on, Wylder Street they'd been told, wasn't bustling, but noises from elsewhere in town filtered through. She heard the tinkling of piano music, horses, and an occasional gunshot. She caught Race's hand and moved closer.

"Down a ways from the jail is Doc Hansen's office." He pointed, continuing the tour and crossing a side street. "This here is Sidewinder Lane. One of the vacant properties I mentioned is down there. It's one the bank owns; I can show you tomorrow; I don't have the key with me now." He hurried them along, though Millie craned her next to catch a glimpse of her potential new home.

"This is the Wylder Mercantile; only place in town to get most anything. Wylders run an upright business. Though they have a bit of a monopoly," he murmured under his breath. They reached the point where Wylder Street ended and ran into an adjacent street. "This is Buckboard Alley. Across the way is Culpepper's Boarding house. It's not been open long, but I hear good things. You get two meals a day with your room, so that's a convenience."

Race nodded at a two-story building across from the mercantile. "That the only hotel in town? Isn't it a conflict of interest having the boardinghouse so close?"

"The Wylder Hotel has more rooms, but the meals aren't as good and cost extra. I imagine Eulalia Culpepper and her husband picked her spot to attract hotel overflow. Well, that's all the important parts of town. I'll leave you here to make room arrangements. Come by the bank tomorrow and we'll get everything else sorted." He shook Race's hand again and waddled back up the street.

Race turned to Millie with a scowl. A lock of black hair fell over one eye and he shoved it back with his hand. "Wife?"

She flinched. He never used sharp tones with her. She straightened her spine and looked him in the eye. "I'm your wife. I will no longer be introduced as your sister, *Horace*."

"This isn't what we discussed. What about the annulment?" He glanced around, but no one was within earshot.

"Seems like you're the only one discussing that. I'm your wife and I want to stay your wife." She added a hesitant foot stomp. They usually discussed disagreements and rarely argued. She'd never seen Race lose control, but she didn't want to find out what happened when he was pushed too far.

He'd let go of her hand at some point and now grabbed her arm, pulling her closer so he could lower his voice. "What if I don't want a wife?"

His tone sent excited shivers up her spine, while his words made her nose tingle with ready tears. "You've had a wife for the past six years whether you wanted one or not. When you took me on, you leg-shackled yourself to me for life."

"That wasn't my intent. Do you know what would have happened if I'd left you there?" He pulled her closer still and his familiar, comforting scent enveloped her.

"This isn't a discussion for the street. Let's find a room so we can settle in." She glanced toward the mercantile where two cowboys had emerged.

He released her abruptly. "You're right, but we will be discussing this later. Do you have a preference where we stay?"

Race could turn his emotions off like a switch. "I'm ready for some good food. Let's try the boarding house."

They waited for some horses to pass, then crossed to Culpepper's. A young woman with bright red hair and sharp, suspicious eyes answered their knock.

"We're looking for rooms," Race said.

She eyed Race up and down then did a quick scan of Millie. "You married? I don't hold with no fiddling around. If that's what you want, you head on over to the social club."

The food must be exceptionally good for anyone to put up with Culpepper's rude proprietress. Race ground his teeth together, he wouldn't have anything left but nubs before too long. Pretty paint and neat trim work couldn't make up for the home's snarling owner. The woman must have thought she was a sporting lady. Race was older; she couldn't do anything about it, but Millie didn't think she looked like a soiled dove.

"We're married," he growled. "But we need two rooms." Race's fists were clenched at his side.

The woman looked hard at Millie this time before answering. "I got one. Dinner's at five; it's almost over. Breakfast at six." She turned to lead them back in.

Millie started to follow, but Race held her back.

"We really need two. We'll try the hotel. Thank you for your time." He pulled Millie down the steps with him.

"None my business." The woman turned, flipping the long red braid over her shoulder and slammed the door.

Millie pulled on Race's hand, stopping him before they reached the street. "These are people we are going to be seeing around town, Race. They're going to think we're strange. We can share a room. We're *married*, for goodness sake!"

Chapter 4

Race's jaw ached. He stalked to the livery to retrieve their belongings after settling a pouting Millie in her room. Why couldn't she understand that he just wanted to free her from him. Why did she continue to torment him with the possibility of a life he didn't deserve? He'd had his chance at happiness, once. Millie deserved more than a shell of a man.

Unfortunately, the part of Race's brain that didn't agree with his plans had been very persistent of late. It tried to convince him he could be a good husband to Millie and his brokenness and age didn't make a difference. It tried to tell him he offered more in experience and material wealth then any younger buck out there. That part of his brain also told him what the rest of his brain suspected; brotherly did not accurately describe what he felt for Millie.

She needed to have a chance at real love, not feelings that developed out of gratitude, proximity, and hero worship. He'd have to sit her down and explain it to her in a way she'd accept. He'd hoped to be able to settle for good in Wylder and quit with the nomadic life he'd forced her to live. That couldn't happen now, not with people thinking they were married. Millie's impetuousness ruined his plans. He'd planned to get a quiet annulment and then start interviewing worthy beaus for his 'sister'. He didn't know what all it would entail, but since the marriage hadn't been consummated, he hoped it could be easily undone. Now, they would have to move on before he could set her up with a new husband. The thought brought a familiar queasiness to his stomach. The feeling he used to get when he thought of being married to Millie, now surface when he thought of anyone else being with her.

He kicked at the dirt in frustration. When he looked up, he faced the small Catholic church. How fortuitous. He climbed the steps and tried the door; locked. He circled to the alley behind the building. The church backed up to a tobacco shop, a diner, and what appeared to be a saloon. The combinations of aromas didn't do anything to ease his roiling stomach. He leaned his back against the church and slid to the ground.

"Lord, what am I supposed to do?"

"'e doesn't usually answer me either."

Race shot to his feet. Before him stood a woman, maybe a year or two older than Millie. Her light brown hair was haphazardly scraped away from her face into a loose bun. Her red-rimmed blue eyes were bright against her blotchy, fair skin.

"Ma'am. Sorry, I didn't know this was anyone's spot. I sought a bit of solace."

"Aye, I gathered as much. You're welcome to it. I often come seeking the same." She leaned on the wall several feet from him.

"I'm Race Lowery. My, ah, wife and I are new to town." He started to offer his hand, but the woman's wary demeanor made him keep his distance. "I'll leave you to it, then. Have a nice night." He slipped past her and headed to the livery.

When he returned to the hotel, Millie opened her door enough for Race to slip her bag through, then shut it in his face. They'd both had a taxing day. There's be no relationship discussion that night. He brought plates of food for them both from the dining room. She accepted hers with a brief 'thank you' and closed the door again.

Race rolled into bed expecting to be asleep in seconds but instead ended up assessing his life until the wee hours of the morning. He thought about Rosemary and Mary Catherine. Their images faded from his mind now that he didn't keep their daguerreotypes by his bedside anymore. Did he still miss them? He wasn't sure. He still felt like he'd failed them, but pain no longer came with the memories.

Rosemary would have been ashamed of his behavior. He'd failed her in death by not living well. Millie really had saved him in that sense. After their marriage, he set aside the bottle and started making an effort to atone for messing up her life. Not that it had been that great to begin with. He wanted to be an example of a good man, the type of man she should be with. He wanted to show her not all men were like Otis and the fellas who visited Bethesda. In his efforts, somewhere along the way, he'd actually turned back into a good man. At least on the outside.

On the inside, Race was still the man who failed his first family, the drinker and the gambler. He was the man who married a girl less than half his age. Regardless of his reasons, at the time, it went against his moral code. Now, as the broken-down man having impure thoughts about that same girl, there was not a thing in the world stopping him from going into the next room and ravaging her. Hell, she even wanted him to; she may not be experienced but she expressed her interest clear enough. His need to protect Millie from himself was the only thing standing in his way. It became hard to continue to think of her as his sister when the word 'wife' had been repeated so many times that day.

****

Millie was trying the *silent treatment*, but she didn't know if she was doing it right or if Race even noticed. She once heard ladies discussing it while working the counter in Iowa City. It sounded simple enough to just not talk. It wasn't easy at all, though. She and Race never played those kinds of games and she'd grown used to talking with him over the evening meal. She missed him already.

Ignoring him didn't seem to be working anyway. He hadn't wanted to share a room with her anyway. She needed to figure out a different tact. She wished Bethy lived closer. What she needed most was an older woman to guide her and share all the secrets of womanhood she'd missed out on being raised by Race during those years. Now here she was, a full-fledged woman without a clue as to how to gain her husband's affections; other than behaving like a whore. She saw plenty of that type of behavior in the towns they'd lived in, but never saw a *wife* act that way. She needed to find some women friends.

She followed a few steps behind Race on the way to the bank. He'd stop so she could walk with him but would fall behind again after a few steps. She admired the mercantile, bigger than the one they'd owned in Iowa City, but smaller than Santa Fe. She scanned

Wylder Street, on the lookout for respectable women. Traffic clogged the street while wagons and horses churned-up road dust. People crossed to and fro, going about their business and avoiding the horse patties scattered about their paths. The difference from the previous evening astounded her.

She could pick out cowboys and businessmen by their attire. Ranchers were a little cleaner than cowhands. Several men with unkept hair and beards had leather pouches hanging from their belts; miners perhaps. A man with a star on his vest chatted with another outside the doctor's office. There were very few women. In fact, there were none other than herself. Every face turned toward her. A wagon full of wood planks nearly plowed down a man who stopped in the middle of the street.

"Millie, come on." Race was waiting on her again and beginning to lose patience.

"Why is everyone looking at us?"

"Probably because we're new. Stay next to me. If those men think you're unattached they'll never leave you alone." Race reached for her hand, voluntarily for the first time.

She was so surprised she almost forgot to reply with a haughty comeback. "Isn't that what you want, to foist me off on someone else?"

"Not the like of any of them. Please behave yourself when we meet Mr. Mountroy."

Millie pulled her hand from Race's grasp. "I'm not a child. I know how to behave in social situations and how to talk to people. I used to run a mercantile, remember?"

He sighed and ran a hand through his hair. "I

thought you did until you pulled that stunt yesterday."

Millie stopped walking and put her hands on her hips. "That was no stunt. That was telling the God's honest truth. I don't want to start off in our new home with a lie."

Race spoke through gritted teeth. "Once again, this is not the place for this discussion. Table it until we get back to the hotel."

"As you wish." Millie took Race's hand again because he allowed it. She wasn't going to let her frustration with him keep her from enjoying the rare experience.

****

They passed the nearly completed Vincent Hotel and found Mr. Mountroy waiting for them outside the bank.

"Good morning, good morning, I trust you slept well." Alfred pumped Race's hand. "I received some good news this morning. The Vincent should be complete in the next two weeks, and I'll get most of the crew back to build my bank. Come, let me show you my clock."

The banker was content to do most of the talking, to Race's relief. Between his lack of sleep and Millie's close proximity, his own words were slow to form. He followed the man into the bank. The younger Mountroy, seated at the desk, straightened importantly when they entered. Race nodded to the man as he walked by but noticed his eyes immediately strayed to Millie. With a frown, Race reached for her hand and pulled her into a back room behind Alfred.

"Isn't she beautiful? It's almost identical to the one in St. Louis, you know. Nothing says respectability like a clock outside your establishment. It tells people you are a professional business and time is important." He laughed. "In our case, time is money."

Race ignored the man's rambling and examined the three-foot-tall monstrosity sitting on the table. It was one of the ugliest models E. Howe carried. The bracket clock had a griffin sitting on a block base. The griffin's beak held an overlarge pocket watch so people could tell the time from the front. Perched on the griffin's head was a crown holding another clock. Equally wide as the mythical beast, it was one and a half times as tall. The double-sided clock showed the time to folks traveling in both directions. It was topped with a feathered urn copper finial. The griffin itself was intricately carved from its gripping claws and individual feathers to its indignant, heavy-browed expression. Probably at having a pocket watch hanging from its mouth and a giant clock on its head. It was a masterpiece in excess and completely inappropriate for the streets of Wylder.

"Model number ninety, a classic," Race agreed without really agreeing. The thing's beauty was subjective. He personally thought it terrifying in addition to being ugly. He pitied the townsperson who might come upon it, unsuspecting, in the dark. "It will need a fairly stout beam to hold it up and it will stick out into the walkway about two feet."

"Marvelous! I want it to really stand out." Alfred's eyes gleamed as he gazed lovingly at his clock.

"Can I see your building plans? Ideally, this model should be mounted right above eye level. Any higher and you won't be able to read the smaller clock without craning your neck."

Alfred unrolled a tube of blueprints on the table. Examining the blue drafting papers he'd heard about excited him more than seeing the actual plans. He bent to get a closer look at the doorframe specifications.

Millie wandered over, bringing her unique scent with her, and leaned over the table next to Race. "You're going to put bars on the windows? It's gonna look like a jail."

"Only the lower ones, to prevent theft."

Race pointed to the middle of the paper. "If you make this beam shorter, you can add another here, perpendicular to it, sticking out about two feet. That's the only place I can make it work." He didn't add that it would look foolish. He stepped back from the table to distance himself from his wife.

"Fine idea. I'll have my draftsman adjust the plans." Alfred re-rolled the blueprints and slid them into a tube. "Now how about I show you that property?"

They followed him back through the front, where Fredrick waited on a man in a dusty, wide-brimmed hat. Race tipped his own felt derby in acknowledgment and thought for the hundredth time he ought to trade-in his battered city hat for something more common to the area. He'd lived west of the Mississippi for almost seven years. It was time he conceded he'd never return to Boston.

"Hold down the fort, Freddie," Alfred called over his shoulder, missing the sneer that flashed across his son's face. He led them past the Vincent and down Sidewinder Lane. "It's right around the corner, making it a short commute for you as long as you're working for me. Convenient to the mercantile for the little woman, too." He stopped in front of a two-story house.

"We want to run a clock and dress shop out of it as well as live there." Millie stared up at the weathered white house.

Ignoring her, Alfred began listing the property's other amenities. "This home was built by the Wylders when they first came to town. They ran the mercantile out of the lower level until they built the bigger store. They rented the space out and eventually sold it to a man who thought to sell fossils, if you can believe it. He relocated somewhere near Medicine Bow and defaulted on his loan. I've been trying to unload it for a couple years now. It's a fine property but no one is looking for anything this big."

"The location is good. Shall we take a look inside, Millie?" The heat from his wife's glare burned imaginary holes in Alfred's back. This was going to be her home even more so than his. He wanted her to help make the decision about it.

Millie stalked up the front steps and waited on the porch for the men to join her. Alfred fitted the key and led them in.

"It's a bit dusty. I haven't checked it in a while. This is the biggest room, right in front. There's an office and a good-size storeroom you could rent out as an apartment with little effort."

Race wandered through the space while Millie poked her nose into the other two rooms.

"The upstairs is where the Wylders lived. It's a regular size home with two bedrooms, dining room, kitchen, and parlor. Right fancy."

Millie returned to Race's side. "Can we see the upstairs?"

Alfred led them upstairs via an interior staircase. Exterior stairs on both the north and south sides of the house would make it easy to divide the upstairs into two apartments later if they chose.

"There's some furniture. Nothing a good beating won't restore." Alfred waited while Race and Millie peeked in all the rooms.

"What do you think? Do want to see what else there is?" Race asked while they were on the other side of the space from Alfred.

Millie bit her lip. "We know how busy mercantiles can be, especially if there's only one in town. This is a good location for our businesses."

"You seem hesitant. What's wrong?" He resisted the urge to touch her arm.

"It's an awful lot of space. I don't know how to live not being cramped."

Race smiled. "That's a good problem to have."

"Can we afford it?" Her hopeful gray eyes stared into his.

"Almost. But we can take out a small mortgage."

Alfred appeared behind them. "This is the only commercial property with living quarters attached. Anything else, and you're looking at two mortgages for your shop and your home. But I can direct you to the land office if you'd like to look at something else. This is the only property in town the bank currently owns. Everything else are homesteads outside the city proper."

Race peered out the window into the back yard they shared with the mercantile. There was quite a bit of space. "We have a lot of options with this place, Mills. We can turn the storage room into an apartment to let out. If there isn't a demand for dresses, you can take in laundry. There's space for lines out back."

"I trust your judgment in this. Let's get it." She graced him with a beatific smile, the kind he'd do well to avoid.

Chapter 5

Millie unpacked her trunk in the smaller bedroom. She didn't plan to be there long, so she'd insisted Race take the bigger room with the bigger bed. They'd spent the past few days scouring the floors and hauling furniture and mattresses up and down the stairs for beating and airing. She couldn't wait to fall into bed, alone...for now.

She took out a small bundle of letters. Bethesda gave them to her when they'd left Scotts Bluff a little over a week ago. She'd completely forgotten them. As usual, it contained missives to her from Bethy as well as letters her mother wrote to Bethy from Savannah. *Savannah, where her mother lived with her new husband and new daughter.* Not so new anymore she supposed, but her mother was frozen in time, the way she looked sixteen years ago when she left.

She untied the ribbon and pulled out the top letter.

Dearest Beth,

I am quite ill. As you can see, my hand shakes as I write this. Philip is hopeful I'll recover but the doctors are not so optimistic. This may be my last opportunity to thank you again for telling me about my daughter over the years. I'm glad she's found a worthy husband and gotten to see the world beyond Scotts Bluff. Winnifred loved hearing all about her sister's travels.

My daughter is a great comfort to me, but I can't

stop thinking about the one I left behind. Leaving Mildred is my greatest regret. It eats away at me as surely as this disease. I am relieved she has thrived despite my abandonment. Otherwise, I could not have lived with myself. My strong and independent girl owes everything to you. You were the mother I could not stay and be.

I love you, my friend. Please tell Millie I love her with all my heart. There will be no more letters but from Winnifred to tell you of what arrangements have been made. It may be callous of me to speak of my imminent death. I no longer have the patience for pretty words or sparing feelings (much to Philip's embarrassment at times).

Thank you and be well.

Annie Chambers

Millie carefully refolded the letter. She didn't know how to feel about the mother who only ever wrote pretty words and sentiments about her abandoned first daughter. A tear escaped and dripped onto the envelope. Her mother left her, her father didn't want her, even her husband didn't want her around. She would unlikely have the opportunity to speak to her and ask her why. She knew of course. Her father had been abusive. She even understood her mother's reasons. But what her mind understood, her heart struggled with.

As they'd traveled to Santa Fe, all those years ago, she'd read every letter in the packet Bethy had given her. She read how much her mother missed her, yet on the same page her mother would write about Winnifred's antics and accomplishments. Winnifred. The sister who stole her mother's love, stole Millie's life.

Millie wrapped the ribbon around the envelopes and put them in her trunk, not bothering to read the rest. She knew all she needed to. She could finally close that chapter of her life and start fresh. She no longer needed to try to live a life her absent mother would be sorry she missed. She no longer needed to think about the woman at all. As for the sister she'd never met, her mother's death would sever her only tie to the girl.

While Millie cleaned upstairs, Race made the downstairs ready to house their businesses and did the preliminary work required to turn the storage room into an apartment one day. His quick tread sounded on the interior stairs.

"Millie, come on down. I want to show you the sign before I hang it." Race grinned, looking pleased with himself.

"Already? I'm coming." She followed him down the stairs. They'd been so busy she'd forgotten to work on his seduction as they fell back into their comfortable work patterns. It was time to figure out her next step.

Race accomplished much while she'd worked upstairs. The wood floors shone, and sun streamed through the clean windowpanes. He'd unpacked the clocks and yard goods they brought from Iowa City and placed them on shelves. He turned the office into his clock repair shop and placed a large table in the main room for laying out fabric and patterns.

"You've done so much, Race. It's wonderful!" Millie spun in a slow circle admiring her workspace.

"I'm glad you like it. This table and chairs are for your customers to sit and wait. I purchased a small stove for the storage room apartment. You'll be able to use it to serve tea. If you'd like, that is."

"This won't be like running a mercantile at all, will it?" She turned to him.

"No. This is a specialty shop. You'll have more select clientele. You know, E. Howe is selling stitching machines now. It would help you work faster."

"Faster isn't always better quality. I wouldn't know what to do with one of those fancy machines, but I thank you for thinking of it. Now, show me your sign." She headed for the front door.

"*Our* sign. Come on." He opened the door and ushered her out. Propped on two chairs, the freshly painted store sign read 'Lowery's Frocks and Clocks'."

Millie covered her mouth. "Race! It's beautiful You have hidden talents." The letters were all the same size and straight. The L, F, and C were a little more decoratively done. They'd be the envy of the other businesses. "I thought we were going to call it Lowery's Clock and Dress Shop."

"I started to, but then this idea came to me. I wanted it to be special." He shrugged.

"It will be special. I can't wait to open for business." She approached him and placed a hand on his arm, pleased he'd created something suggesting permanence. "This is where we'll start our new life."

Race moved away from her hand. "I'll ask Fredrick to help me hang it tonight and we can open for business tomorrow."

Millie sighed. If opening the shop would help her meet other women, it couldn't happen soon enough.

****

"I hear'd you was gonna take laundry." The crusty miner plunked a stinking sack on Millie's worktable.

"We are not prepared to do so at this time. I make

47

dresses for women and shirts or pants for men. I will also do mending." Millie slid the bag toward the man. "But only clean clothes."

"Well, I got some of that. Guess I'll go wash em up in the creek afore I bring em back." He slung the sack over his shoulder.

"With soap!" Millie called as exited.

Race poked his head out of the workshop. "Everything all right out here?"

"Yes. I turned away another miner asking about laundry. Who is telling them that anyway?" Millie smacked an insect on the table where the sack had been.

"Maybe Mr. Mountroy. We talked about it as a future possibility while we were all upstairs. If he mentioned, it to one person…"

"The whole town knows. Yes, I'm aware. Every person who's come through the door seems to know who we are, where we're from, and what color socks you're wearing."

Race looked at his feet and Millie laughed. They both looked up as two young women entered.

Though a little older than her own twenty years, Millie prepared herself to make friends of the pair.

Race nodded at the newcomers. "Good day, ladies."

"We are so excited to have a dress shop in town. Wylder's only ever carries plain, small-sized ready-made dresses." The woman stepped to the counter and extended her hand to Race. "I'm Una Barlow and this is Sarah Holt."

Race shook both women's hands while Millie made introductions.

"I'm Millie Lowery and this is my husband, Race.

It's a pleasure to meet you. I'm glad to finally meet someone who isn't a miner." She shook each of their hands as well.

"I'll be in my workshop. Nice to meet you." Race disappeared into the other room.

"I can't believe your husband lets you help run a business." Sarah's gaze swept around the shop. "Clocks and dresses, an interesting combination. My husband, Rick has a pocket watch that keeps losing time. Can your Race fix that?"

"I'm sure he can," Millie replied. Sarah was everything Millie wished to be. She was tall, slender, and had hair the color of ripe wheat. Her eyes were a true blue, rather than Millie's dull gray. She bet Sarah could even make the mercantile's ready-made dresses look good.

Una reminded her of Bethy in her younger years. Taller and heavier than Millie, she carried it with confidence. Her full bosom strained at her bodice and her hips flared out from her waist in a way men seemed to like. She'd pulled her dark brown hair back from her rounded face in a sleek twist. Neither woman looked like they belonged in an upstart town like Wylder.

Una craned her neck to see Race in his work room then turned to Millie and lowered her voice. "You're here just in time. I am increasing and will need a whole new wardrobe."

Sarah sucked in a breath. "Una! Congratulations! You and Ambrose have been trying for so long." She hugged her friend.

"Mmm, yes. It's been a trial for certain." Una's eyes flicked away from Sarah.

"Congratulations, ma'am. I look forward to making

some dresses for you." Millie smiled, tamping down the jealousy pinching her heart.

"Oh, please. You must call us Sarah and Una. There are so few women in this town, we shall be fast friends." Sarah placed her hand on Millie's.

Millie smiled with relief. This was easier than she'd hoped. "Then you must call me Millie. Do you live close by?"

"I don't," Sarah said. "My husband has a horse ranch outside of town, but we come in about once a week."

"Otherwise, you'd go crazy!" Una laughed, brushing Sarah's arm. "My Ambrose has investments here in town. He owns a little bit of a lot of places." She laughed again. "We live near the boarding house. Have you met Eulalia Culpepper?"

"Briefly." Millie did not want to discuss her meeting with the strange woman.

"Sour grapes, that one," Sarah said. "She's not friendly with us; she thinks she's better, somehow. She's married, but she runs roughshod over her husband. No one knows much about her and she's so rude to me when I see her in town, I don't even care."

"Who needs her when you've got me?" Una asked. "And now Millie, too." She beamed at Millie. She glanced toward the front window. "Speaking of sour grapes."

A thirtyish-looking woman entered the shop and stopped short at the sight of Millie's customers. She focused on Millie. "I see you're busy with customers. I'll come back later." She quickly turned.

"No, wait!" Millie rushed around the table and caught her arm before she could run off. "Please. I want to meet all the women in town. I'm Millie Lowery. I run the dress shop. What can I do for you?"

The woman glanced over Millie's shoulder at the other women. "Una. Sarah. Hello."

"Hello, Sally. How are you?" Sarah asked sweetly.

"I'm fine, thank you."

Millie didn't think the woman sounded fine. She held her body rigid, ready to bolt at a moment's notice.

"Millie, this is Sally Smithers. Her husband is caretaker for the Episcopal church. How *is* Robert these days? I haven't seen him in ages," Una purred.

"You haven't seen him or anyone else cause you haven't been at church," Sally snapped, then pursed her lips.

"I've been feeling poorly lately; in the mornings. But I'm there in spirit." Una rubbed her stomach, drawing Sally's eye. "Ambrose was pleased with the fence Robert put in and the roof hasn't leaked since he repaired it. I know I appreciate having a younger man available to take care of the things Ambrose isn't able to anymore."

Sally blanched and turned to Millie. "I wanted to see if you took in mending. I have poor joints and would like to turn over the task."

Millie nodded. "I do."

"Fine. I'll come back later." Sally escaped out the door before Millie could say another word.

"What was that all about?" she asked her new friends.

"Sally Smithers is a hateful old thing." Una sniffed.

The woman hurried down the street. Millie wouldn't have described her as hateful. "She doesn't look that old."

"She's not. She's really more sad than hateful," Sarah said.

"Why is that?" Millie asked, walking back around her table.

"She's barren, that's why." Una flicked invisible dust from her sleeve. "She can't conceive so she's taken on the mantle of oldness. It's a shame, too. Her husband is a mighty attractive man. Such a waste."

Millie pondered how she'd feel in Sally's position. "She should be happy she has a husband instead of being miserable about the things she can't have." She lowered her voice a fraction. "I could bear anything with Race at my side."

Sarah nodded in agreement.

"Enough of that. What shall we do next week when you're in town, Sarah? Shall we take Millie to tea?" Una asked.

Sarah exploded into giggles. "Una jests. There's no place to go for tea in this dirty town except her own parlor."

"What about the Social Club?" Millie heard the name mentioned around town. It sounded quite fancy.

The women froze, then started in on a new round of giggling.

Millie looked from on to the other. "What?"

Sarah reached over and patted her arm. "Honey, the Social Club is a brothel."

****

1848

"Bethy, please! I just want ta borrow a little lip paint and eye powder. You've got enough up here for three people," Millie pleaded.

Bethesda, the prostitute who'd been a mother to

Millie for the past ten years, turned away from her mirror. "That is not the point, ducky." She cupped Millie's chin with her hand. "You are beautiful without all the gunk on your face."

Millie sulked. "You wear it."

"Mmm, but you don't have any years to hide like I do."

"Hows am I gonna look good to catch a husband?"

Bethesda frowned. "What your daddy is doin' is wrong; you're too young. I tried to talk him out of it, but he's plumb weary of being responsible for anyone but himself." She snorted. "As if he had any part in the raisin of ya."

"He's letting me serve dinner t'night at the table."

"I know it. I'll try to get down there to keep an eye on things, but Friday night is my busiest. Even worse since Bella Rae quit town. Be yourself and hopefully your daddy will pick someone for ya who ain't too ornery." A knock sounded at the door. "That'd be Silas. He's early. Git on down the back steps and I'll check on you in the morning." She stood and adjusted her bust and skirts before walking to the door.

"Good night, Bethy. I'll see you in the morning." Millie quietly scooped two small jars off the table left out the back door.

Chapter 6

It gladdened Race's heart to hear Millie laughing with the other women and made a point to not listen to their conversation. He didn't know if Millie had ever made friends her own age. Living as his sister in the other town made female friendships difficult. Other girls her age were either busy wives or daughters trying to find husbands. Not forming friendships helped them both avoid awkward situations. He never told her about the women who flirted with him, nor about the boy he'd denied permission to court her. It was past time for them to resolve their relationship and move on. The thought jarred him.

"Dang it!" He fumbled a gear and dropped his truing caliper on the floor where he accidently kicked it under his desk. He'd have to start over with the repair job.

Millie poked her head into the office. "What's wrong, Race?"

He retrieved the tool and stood up. "Nothing, Millie. Just butterfingers. I'm going to step out for a bit. Will you be all right by yourself?"

"I'll be fine. I'm going to make tea for Una and Sarah."

Race waited for Millie to move out of the doorway before edging past. "Good afternoon, ladies. Enjoy your visit." He grabbed his hat and went out the front door.

He crossed the street to the alley behind the Vincent House. The shortcut brought him almost to the back door of the Catholic Church. He circled to the front; this time the door opened at his touch.

He entered and pulled the door closed behind him. A simple octagonal baptismal font was positioned directly to his left. Touching the water, he genuflected and made the sign of the cross. Fourteen oil lamp sconces burned on each side of the windowless sanctuary, illuminating the stations of the cross. The smell of incense lingered, permeating the wood. The building was simple compared the Catholic churches in the east. Rectangular in shape, the traditional cruciform was accomplished by pew placement instead of transepts. Also missing was the domed apse and confessionals, though Race noted a shriving pew set aside near the pulpit.

The table beyond the lectern held a stone statue of the Virgin. Race went there and lit a reed off of a lighted votive. He used it to light two other votives in the rows before him. He said prayers for Rosemary and Mary Catherine, then left a three-cent piece in the donation box.

He turned. A woman sat in one of the pews. He didn't know if she'd come in while he lit the candles or had been there all along. She looked like the same woman he encountered outside the last time he came. A balding man in priest's robes emerged from a door behind the pulpit.

"Mrs. McCarthy." His voice echoed through the sanctuary, giving the illusion of a bigger space. "Has your situation altered?"

"No, Father." Her voice was clear and unashamed.

The priest didn't say another word; he simply stared at her intently.

The woman, Mrs. McCarthy, sighed and rose from the pew. She gathered her shawl in her arms and walked toward the door, head held high. She paused at the last station and performed the familiar rituals before exiting. She never acknowledged Race's presence.

The priest turned to Race. "Good afternoon. I'm Father Donahue, how may I serve you?"

Race shook the man's offered hand. "Race, ah Horace Lowery, Father. My wife and I are new in town."

He smiled. "Ah, yes. The clock and dress shop. I have a mantel clock I plan to bring by."

"I'd be pleased if you did, Father."

"Are you and your wife wishing to transfer to our congregation?"

Race shuffled his feet. "I have a situation I'd like to discuss with you." They sat in a front pew and Race explained his previous Episcopalian candidacy and subsequent transfer of faiths when he married his first wife. He told how his current marriage came about and his reasons for wanting to set Millie free."

The priest listened without asking any questions until Race finished. "I can't give you an annulment because you weren't married in a Catholic church. Hearing your story, I don't know that an annulment is the best course of action. I can't absolve you for your feelings for your wife, son. They aren't sinful."

Race shifted in the pew like a chastised child. He knew there were ways of sinning that didn't feel sinful. He didn't know how to reconcile something that felt sinful but wasn't.

Father Donahue continued, "In fact, denying your wife your body is as much a sin as if it were the other way around. I will absolve you of your guilt over the death of your first family. It's arrogant of you to think you had any control over that situation. As a former candidate for a clerical position in any denomination, you should know this." He frowned at Race. "I think you have been away from church for too long and it sounds like your bride is completely unchurched. Come to one of the masses this weekend. We'll see you set to rights." Father Donahue rose, signaling the end of the audience.

Race remained seated. "I'll let myself out in a few minutes if that's all right with you, Father. Thank you for your counsel."

"Bless you, son. I hope you find the answers you need rather than the ones you're looking for." He turned and walked back to the little room behind the pulpit.

The sun nearly blinded him when he stepped back outside.

"Who are you, den?"

Race whipped his head to the right. The woman from earlier leaned against the building. She still seemed wary, so he didn't offer his hand. "I'm Race Lowery. My wife and I opened a dress shop near the mercantile. I also repair clocks."

She nodded, processing the information. "Father Donahue is a good priest, but a lettle bet pretentious. Not very accepting 'o folks trying to get by. Likes dem stayin' to the straight and narrow."

"I'll keep that in mind. What's your name?"

She eyed him, considering. "Aoife McCarthy."

"A pleasure. Do you and your husband live in

town?"

"Widow McCarthy," she corrected. "It's nice to meet you, Mr. Lowery. Welcome to Wylder." She pushed herself off the building and started walking south.

What an odd woman. She looked to be close in age to Millie; much too young to be widowed. He recalled the strange interaction between her and the priest. For some reason the man didn't welcome the mourning sister in faith. Curiosity aside, he'd concerns of his own and Aoife was none of his business.

He set off to see if the Episcopal church was open. Maybe the preacher there could offer him a solution. The Catholic church visit left him spiritually dissatisfied in addition to being unhelpful.

He nodded to the men loitering outside the land office then detoured to the livery to check on his team. Chet and young Jackson were busy with the owners of two wagons loaded with furniture and household goods. Wylder might soon be as bustling as Mr. Mountroy claimed. Not wanting to be underfoot, he continued to the church.

St. Joseph's doors and windows were all propped open, taking advantage of the spring breezes. Inside, a woman wrote on a blackboard and four students of varying ages copied numbers on their individual slates.

"If you're looking for the preacher, you'll have a bit of a wait. He rides the circuit and won't be back for a month." A man about Race's age stood by the well. He'd raised the bucket and took a long drink using the dipper.

"Race Lowery. New to town." He offered his hand.

The man wiped his mouth on his sleeve and shook

Race's hand. "Robert Smithers, deacon, caretaker, and everything in between. My wife and I keep up the rectory." He pointed to the small house next to the church. "Digging a new privy today. What can I do for you, Race Lowery?"

Women would probably consider Rob Smithers attractive. His smile and friendly manner made him easy company for men as well. Race's unusual marital situation made him avoid anything other than casual acquaintances in the past. It would be difficult to be friends with an unmarried man but refuse to let him court his 'sister'. Friendships with married men would lead to 'couples' activities and shared confidences. Both invited awkwardness.

"Robert?" A tiny woman rounded the corner of the church. "Oh! I didn't know you had company."

"Sal, come and meet Race Lowery. He and his wife are new in town. Race, this is my wife, Sally." Robert pulled his wife to his side and kissed the top of her head.

Race smiled. Her voice was familiar, and he thought she might have stopped by the shop earlier. "Nice to meet you, ma'am." He tipped his hat.

Sally tensed in her husband's arms. Her eyes narrowed. "I met your wife earlier. She was visiting with Una and Sarah." She stepped away from her husband. "You're new in town, so you won't know this, but as a Christian woman, I feel I must speak out. Sarah Holt is a good sort but she's not very discerning in her female friends. You'd do well to keep your wife," She glanced at her husband, then raked her eyes over Race's form. "And yourself away from Una. She's a bad influence and she's loose to boot."

Robert coughed. "Now, Sal. You don't want to be accused of spreading gossip."

Sally glared at him. "Don't I? Don't you dare defend her to me."

Robert took her hand and pulled her back to him. Using both his hands, he began gently rubbing her knuckles. She closed her eyes and winced.

"I wouldn't. Forget about Una." He let go of her hand and began ministering to the other one.

Eyes still closed, she said, "Until the next ladies' auxiliary meeting. She's never gonna be out of my hair, Robert. And now she's pregnant."

This time, Robert stiffened. He returned her hand to her side. "Why were you looking for me?"

Sally opened her eyes. The pain displayed in them seemed far deeper than purely physical. "I was checking to see what time you thought you'd be in for dinner."

"How about seven?"

"That'll be fine." She turned to Race. "Nice to meet you. I hope you enjoy living in Wylder." She turned and briskly walked back the way she came.

"Sal!" Robert jogged a few steps to catch up to her. He bent and said something to her while rubbing her back. Then he placed another kiss on her head. She continued on and Robert returned to Race. "We're having trouble conceiving. She gets touchy anytime anyone turns up breeding. It's worse that it's Una." He rubbed the back of his neck.

Race thought it seemed like more than that. This was the type of shared confidence he avoided. He'd keep an eye on the Una situation, though.

"Let me buy you a drink one night." Robert's smile

returned but had dimmed.

"I appreciate the offer, but I tend to make bad decisions when I drink. Try to avoid the hard stuff, but I'll take you up on a cider or soda water if it's available in these parts."

"I understand. I have my share of drink-related regrets. Drinking's the only way I can forget some of my bad decisions anymore." The man focused inward, and the last statement seemed made more to himself. "Sal's not wrong about Una. If you value your marriage, steer clear of her."

"Thanks for the advice. I need to get back."

As Race hurried home he thought about the conversation. He didn't *not* value his marriage. He didn't value it the way a husband ought either, he supposed. He'd never thought about it in those terms, and it made him feel lower than a snake's belly. He'd never do anything to hurt Millie. She didn't understand that an annulment was the best thing he could do for her, if it could even be done. He'd based his whole plan on it. He wouldn't saddle her with the shame of a divorce. This wasn't her fault. But something needed to be done soon, before his resolve weakened and broke.

Chapter 7

Millie turned the sign and locked the shop door. It had been a successful first day, as far as meeting folks, anyway. She planned to start on the pile of mending that evening and an order for a christening dress wouldn't take any time at all to complete.

Una and Sarah stayed until Sarah's husband and adorable little boy came looking for her. Race returned from his errand shortly after and kept to his office the rest of the afternoon.

Millie could hardly keep the grin from her face. Her plan to seduce her husband was starting to take shape. She didn't ask her new friends' advice yet. It was too personal a topic for a first meeting. They would have tea again next week and she'd try to work her questions into the conversation somehow.

First, she would make herself a new dress. All during tea, she studied the lines and cut of Una's dress. Millie was confident she could copy the pattern from memory and make the same sort of thing for herself. She'd never worn anything so low-cut. It seemed daring for everyday wear, but she wanted to appear daring and bold, like Una.

She had an old corset packed away in a trunk; she'd find it to wear with the new dress. Her full bosom embarrassed her, but the new Millie would use it to her advantage.

"Closing time already?" Race came out of his office untying his apron.

"It's five. I'm heading up and start dinner. It was a good day, Race. I'm so happy." It bubbled up inside her, threatening to overflow. She walked over to her husband. Butterflies started playing with the bubbles in her chest. "I want to thank you for everything you've done for me, for us." Before she could doubt herself, she stepped forward and wrapped Race in a hug. Her head only reached his chest, so she mashed her cheek into the placket of his shirt, knowing she'd probably have little, round button imprints on her face.

Race staggered back a half step and coughed, but after a few seconds returned her embrace. She squeezed him tighter, his lips and nose pressed the top of her head. *This was progress*. His hand ran up her back and rested on her bare neck. Gooseflesh erupted down her arms. She grazed her hands up his solid back and the heat of him penetrated through her dress. He emitted a low groan. They'd hugged before, but this was something a bit more stirring. Race released her abruptly and stepped back.

He cleared his throat. "I'm glad you like it here, Mills. I went by the Catholic church while I was out earlier. We won't be able to get an annulment there since we weren't married there, and you aren't Catholic. I'll try the Episcopal preacher when he's back in town."

All Millie's excitement for the day came crashing down around her. Tears pricked the corners of her eyes. "Why are you in such an all-fired hurry to get rid of me?" She gulped in a breath to keep from crying. She *would* have an adult conversation with him about this.

Race sighed and stepped away from her. "Mills, we've talked about this—"

"We have *not*. You've *told* me what you plan to do. You haven't asked me what I want."

"You don't understand. I'm broken, Mills. You deserve a better man than me. You deserve a young man that can give you the best years of his life. I don't have anything left to offer."

Millie stomped her foot. "You don't know what you're talking about. We've been together for six years. I've seen what you consider broken. Race, you've been healing this whole time. And why would I want a younger man? I'm already used to you. I love *you*."

He hung his head. "It doesn't matter how you or I feel. I can't let emotions get in the way of the right thing to do. If we became husband and wife in truth, eventually you'd come to resent me and my moods and you'd be stuck with an old man when you're still in your child-bearing years."

"Argh!" Millie threw her hands in the air. The tears were gone, replaced by frustrated anger. "I'm going upstairs." She stalked toward the staircase.

"I'm going for a walk. Leave the pot on the stove; I'll clean up."

****

Five nights. Five nights Millie sat up mending clothes while Race's dinner chilled on the stove. Five nights he had gone walking to avoid being alone with her. She couldn't wait to meet with Una and Sarah, she needed advice she could start using now.

Her new dress was coming along; she'd chosen a deep garnet polished cotton that looked almost like silk. She thought about using black buttons and piping on it, but decide it too closely resembled some of the designs Bethy used to wear. She settled on mother of pearl buttons and creamy piping and lace. The fabric was all cut and she'd start sewing that day. Race barely left his workshop or looked at her, so she didn't need to worry about hiding it from him. His emotional absence left her bereft.

After Race left them the other day, Una and Sarah explained all about the Wylder County Social Club. She'd been aware of similar establishments in Santa Fe and Iowa City. She'd even been friendly with many of the girls when they came into the mercantile.

This new information intrigued her for two reasons. One, these were women who knew their way around men. They could give her advice. Two, they were also potential clientele for her dress shop. It gave her a way in. After that, she'd play it by ear.

She packed a basket with fabric swatches and some dress sketches.

"Race, I'm running to the post office with a letter to Bethy. Watch the front for me, please." She took a bonnet off the coat hook and tied it on.

Race poked his head out of the workshop. "I can post it for you when I'm out."

"No need. I'm feeling pent-up. I'll stretch my legs a bit and be back."

Race grunted and went back to his work.

It did feel wonderful to be out in the middle of the day. It was warmer than she'd expected and was glad for her bonnet. In the distance she could see snow on the mountains and wondered if it would all melt away in a month when summer arrived.

Delicious aromas emanated from the diner located

catty-cornered from her shop. She and Race never ate out, but the place always seemed to be full. Besides the boarding house and hotel, it was the only place to get a meal you didn't cook yourself.

This early in the day, Old Cheyenne Road didn't look the way Race had described it, largely due to the saloon's quieter daytime clientele. The train platform and stage line buildings were equally deserted.

She did have a letter for Bethy, so stopped at the post office first. Then she circled to the back of the building. She could see the brothel sitting all by its lonesome on the other side of the railroad tracks. She looked to her right and left. No one stirred. Taking a deep bread, she marched with determined steps across the tracks all the way up to the front door.

****

1848

"Why're we going to Santa Fe?" Millie clung to her seat as they bumped their way across trail after barely-there trail.

"I recently obtained ownership of a mercantile there."

"Daddy said you sold clocks."

"I do. I work for E. Howe Clock Company in Massachusetts. I'm somewhat of a traveling merchant, but the job offers me the freedom to move about as I choose."

"You're not going to be able to travel if yer runnin' a shop an have a wife."

Race grimaced. *"This isn't going to be a normal marriage."*

"Why not?"

Race shifted in his seat, trying to put more space

between him and his new wife. "Do you know what goes on between a married man and woman?"

"The woman who raised me is a whore. Course I know."

Race didn't quite know what to make of that statement. He'd met Bethesda briefly. She hadn't been introduced as Millie's mother, but she obviously felt that way toward the girl. The story of Millie's mother had not been shared. "And do you have any feelings like that for me?" He detested having this conversation with a girl who was essentially a child. He turned to give her a searching look, begging her to be honest.

Millie blushed furiously. "I think yer handsome." Her hand snaked up to the hair at her nape. She stopped, then fisted it in her lap.

"That's not the same thing, Millie." He gentled his tone as he would for a nervous animal.

"Why'd you marry me then, if you didn't want a wife?"

Race sighed. "I didn't want to see you misused. You reminded me of my—" But she didn't really remind him of Mary Catherine at all. Technically, he was old enough to have fathered her. His stomach turned, renewing the nausea he'd been battling all morning. "You remind me of my friend's little sister. I didn't like the look of Mr. Monroe. Not that you were given a choice, but it was him or me."

She thought on this for a moment, then said, "I thank you, I s'pose, but I don't know you either. If I'm not to act like your wife, what am I supposed to do?"

"Think of me as a wise older brother."

"Wiser than who? You'd better not say me. You're the one saddled with a wife you don't want."

She wasn't wrong in her assessment. "How about just an older brother, then?"

She eyed him up and down. "So's I can marry someone else someday when boys come a courtin'?"

Regret filled him. He'd trapped them both in his hasty rescue. "We're still a few years off from worrying about that. We'll ford that river when we get to it."

Millie slumped in her seat. "I'm sorry for ruining yer life."

"It was already ruined and on its way to getting worse. You most likely saved my life and gave me something to live for, the next few years. Maybe by the time you're grown, I'll have figured out what to do with the rest of it."

****

A bleary-eyed woman answered Millie's knock on the door of the imposing red house. Though the curtains were drawn on every window, the white-washed shutters gave the home stately appeal. She would not have guessed it to be a brothel. It looked ready to welcome rich men and heads of state. Perhaps maybe it sometimes did.

"Good day. My name is Mildred Lowery and I've recently opened a dress shop in town. I wanted to introduce myself to your, ah, the person in…" She was saved from having to finish when the woman bellowed up the stairwell.

"Amber, Crystal! There's a dressmaker here!" She lifted the basket from Millie's arm. "May I?" It seemed the girl was going to with or without her consent, so she relinquished the basket to her eager hands.

Two more women, presumably Amber and Crystal, clamored down the stairs in disheveled nightclothes and too, fell upon the basket.

Millie raised her voice. "I'm here to see the person in charge of ordering clothing."

One of the girls from upstairs popped her head up. "Sorry. Let me get Miss Addie for you." She hurried off down a dark hallway.

As Millie's eyes adjusted to the dim interior, details began to take shape. Like the exterior of the house, red seemed to be the predominant theme indoors as well. Dark-stained wood floors and wall paneling sucked light from the room, possibly remedied by a wrought iron chandelier handing overhead. The room was lined with upholstered chairs and loveseats in varying shades of red and burgundy. An upright piano sat in the corner with a candelabra on top. The spinning stool tucked in front shone with patina. The Social Club was every bit as elegant as its name suggested. Bethy would have loved it.

"May I help you?"

Millie spun from her gawking. She always assumed the term 'Madam' referred to someone older. It surprised her to find Adelaide Willowby close to her own age. That's where the similarities ended. She appeared to have been in the midst of her morning toilette. A long cornsilk colored coil of hair hung over one shoulder and a wrapper protected her silk jacquard day dress. What the woman lacked in years, she made up for in presence.

She clutched her hands together to keep herself from fidgeting. She was a business owner in her own right. Adelaide Willowby was her equal. She took a deep breath. "I'm Mildred Lowery. I run the new dress shop in town. I'm introducing myself to the local women who might have an interest in my talents."

Addie cocked an eyebrow then flicked her eyes to the other women. "There appears to be some interest. Crystal, settle Miss Lowery in my office." She fixed her eyes on Millie again. "I'll join you in a moment." She turned and disappeared down the hallway.

The woman with pale hair touched her elbow. "This way, ma'am."

Minutes later, Adelaide closed her office door on the women tittering over the basket of swatches and sketches. Wrapper gone, her hair was twisted into an elegant bun and fixed with an ebony comb that match the details on her dark blue dress. She sat down in the tufted wingback chair and crossed one leg over the other. Her fingers tapped on the arm. "I appreciate you stopping by, Miss Lowery. The girls will be glad to not have to suffer their own sewing skills anymore."

Millie fidgeted with her ringless finger. The ring Race gave her six years ago no longer fit. As his 'sister' she had no need of it anyway. "I wondered if you or someone else could help me with a personal matter."

Addie's gaze continued to rest on Millie, never wavering.

"I need the advice of a woman who knows about men," she blurted.

The madam's eyes narrowed. "I want to make one thing very clear. I am not now, nor have I ever been a whore."

This was not going at all like she'd intended. If she offended this woman, she wouldn't get the help she sought nor her business. "I didn't mean to imply as such. I mean, it wouldn't matter to me if you were. I need advice on how to attract a man."

"Nor are we in the business of helping young misses find husbands." Adelaide cut in.

"I already have a husband." Millie noted the dull band on the madam's left hand. "You're a married lady. You can help me." Adelaide was perfect and poised, she carried herself as she imagined a worldly, sophisticated city lady would.

"I don't think I can. I have husband troubles of my own." She glanced pointedly at Millie's naked finger. "If yours isn't treating you right, I can't help you there either."

"He's not treating me at all. That's the problem."

One of Adelaide's blonde eyebrows arched. Before she could speak, a short knock sounded on the door and a young woman came in carrying a tea tray.

"Tea, mum."

"Aoife, what have I told you about the formalities?" Adelaide sighed.

Aoife shrugged. "Mr. Willowby likes it." She set the tray down on a small table.

"Because it makes him feel more important than he is. This is *Mrs.* Lowery. She's opened the dress shop in town. Mrs. Lowery, this is Aoife McCarthy. She's our cook."

Aoife nodded at Millie. "I met your 'usband. 'e's a trooble soul, 'e is."

Adelaide's eyebrow twitched again, and she sat back in her seat.

Millie assessed the woman. "Where did you meet Race?" She didn't like this woman knowing personal things about her husband. She worried Aoife's Irish lilt would remind him of his first wife. She didn't need any more obstacles.

Shelley White

Unaware or perhaps unconcerned with her employer's curiosity and Millie's suspicions, Aoife poured two cups of tea and removed the cloth from a plate of cookies. "Behend de church de first time. Inside de second."

Adelaide groaned. "Sugar cookies again, Aoife? Don't you know any other recipes?"

Millie took a cookie and bit into it, still studying the strange woman. Crisp on the outside and chewy inside, the cookie melted in her mouth. She would gladly eat them every day without complaint.

"It's what's keepin a roof over me 'ead, isn't it?" Aoife turned and swept out of the room, closing the door behind her.

"You needn't worry about Aoife having designs on your husband. She's recently widowed and left with nothing. She came to live here and cook for us and managed to lose her God as well. I suppose He's not lost, but His gatekeeper won't allow her to attend mass, so the results are the same." She wiped the crumbs off her fingers with a linen. "Now back to your problem, Mrs. Lowery. What is it exactly you need?"

"Please call me Millie. Can I speak to you in confidence?" The cookies and tea seemed to have sweetened Addie's disposition toward her.

Adelaide laughed. "I'm no priest, but I promise, what you say will go no further."

Millie took a fortifying sip of tea. "I've never been with my husband intimately."

"I don't understand. He's not gentle with you?"

"We don't share a bed. We've been living as brother and sister for the past six years since married."

72

"He's not actually your brother, is he?" The madam wrinkled her nose in distaste.

"Lord, no! He's a good and honorable man. He married me to save me from an unpleasant and potentially dangerous situation. I was only fourteen, you see. Much too young in his estimation. He wouldn't leave me with my father, so insisted we live as siblings until a time he could get the marriage annulled."

"And how long has this been going on?" She took a sip of her tea.

Millie groaned. "Six years. He's started looking into obtaining an annulment."

"Easier said than done," Addie murmured. "The man must be a saint to eschew marital relations for that long. Has he been going elsewhere?"

Millie's cheeks warmed. "No. He's been mourning his wife and daughter much of that time."

Adelaide tapped a finger to her chin. "I see. And you tolerate each other fairly well?"

"I believe Race has affection for me. He fights it out of a misplaced sense of honor. Otherwise, he wouldn't go out of his way to avoid me. I don't know what to do to force the issue. I haven't had a woman I can talk to till moving here."

"Who else have you spoken with?" Adelaide rose from the chair and crossed to the window.

"Una Barlow and Sarah Holt. I haven't told them anything, we just met." Millie blushed. She hadn't had the same hesitation about sharing her troubles with Adelaide.

Reading her thoughts, Adelaide turned and smiled. "When one deals in the intimate, it makes it easier to broach the subject. If Una could be of any help to you, her husband would not be a frequent visitor to this establishment." She crossed to a bookshelf. "So, you don't know anything about what goes on between a man and a woman?"

Millie blushed. "My mother left when I was young. The women who cared for me entertained men in the above stairs apartment. I know the mechanics. But I know there's more than that between a husband and wife. At least I think there is." She frowned.

"I have decided to help you. I am nothing if not a champion of love." She pulled out several books and brought them to the table.

Millie read the various titles: *Manhood: Causes of its Premature Decline, Burton's Lectures on Female Manners, Man of Pleasure's Kalendar, Aristotle's Masterpiece, Fruits of Philosophy.* Adelaide briefly contemplated each title before setting it aside. She picked up a richly illustrated tome with a title in no language Millie had ever seen before.

"Not ready for that," she mumbled, setting it aside. "Here, try this one. If it doesn't give you some ideas, it will, at least, help your body figure it out on its own." She handed Millie a smaller leather-bound book.

"*Memoirs of a Woman's Pleasure*? But it's written by a man."

"What better way to discover what a man wants? Purely fiction, I assure you, but a good read none the less." She picked up the discarded books and reshelved them. "Farley has a collection of erotic English illustrations. If the book doesn't help, come back and I'll see if I can get my hands on them."

By this time, Millie could feel the burn in her

cheeks. "Th-thank you."

"Now, about the other." Adelaide resettled herself and reclaimed her teacup.

"Other?" Millie set the book in her lap and picked-up her cup as well.

"Yes, the dresses. To start, each girl will need one. How long will they take to complete? Is what you're wearing an example of your work? We'll need something a little more for, um, evening entertaining."

"Oh! If I don't work on anything else, I can finish a dress in three days; four if it's fancy. Yes, I made this. The girls are looking at the sketches. They might like some of those designs. I modeled them after dresses I saw when I lived in Santa Fe."

"Very good. I'll have them come by…"

"Lowery's Frocks and Clocks," Millie supplied.

"Yes, very quaint." She rose, went to the door, and opened it. "Crystal! Bring me Mrs. Lowery's basket, please." She took it and offered it to Millie. "Are all your samples accounted for?"

Millie sorted through the contents, then slid the book under the fabric swatches. "Yes, everything's here."

"Splendid. I'll send the first girl to see you tomorrow. Good luck, Millie." She fingered the sketches. "You might consider sewing one of these designs up for yourself, too. In the interest of furthering your cause."

"Thank you. I'm actually working on something already."

"With that kind of ambition, your husband doesn't stand a chance."

Chapter 8

Race was exhausted. Sleepless nights coupled with his evening walks were catching up to him. The bank construction would be finished soon. When he checked-in with Alfred the previous day, the man assured him the clock installation could happen within the week. It was the only thing keeping him in Wylder, other than waiting on the preacher to come back to town.

He'd learned much about the town during his walks. The same men always headed to the saloon each evening and others took the back way across the tracks to the social club. He passed Ralph Wylder heading home after closing the mercantile and he ran into Robert Smithers outside the Five Star Saloon one evening.

He overheard conversations, too. Rich men in town hoped to entice the railroad into making Wylder a hub instead of just a spur stop. Ambrose Barlow had his finger in that pie as well as being an investor in The Vincent and the new bank. He paid the town's schoolteacher and pushed for a separate school to be built to lure more families to the town.

During all his nocturnal wanderings, his wife was never far from his mind. He didn't know what was worse, being away from home and allowing his mind to wander free or being near her and having to keep a tight rein on his thoughts. Both options made his trousers snug. He feared even leaving Millie for good wouldn't remedy the situation. But he would suffer it if he knew she could move on and be happy. And that thought churned up a whole slew of unwelcome feelings. This night, like the others, he headed to one of the two churches in town. His footsteps took him to the Catholic church, best suited to exorcising his demons.

"You're back. Doon't you 'ave a wife waitin' for you at 'ome?"

He should have expected to run into the mysterious Mrs. McCarthy.

"It's late for you to be out, too." He leaned against the building several feet from where she sat.

"No. Not for de likes o' me."

"I'd feel better if you'd let me escort you home."

She snorted. "An start all kends o' nasty rumors. I don't think so. What brings you 'ere again?"

"I guess you could say I'm trying to expel some demons. What about you?"

"The same, 'cept I'm trying to expel God."

Race pushed away from the wall. "What happened to you? Why did the priest send you away the other day?"

"Well, isn't that none o' your business?" She stared out into the darkness.

He moved closer to her. "Is there anything I can do to help?"

She tilted her head to look up at him. "You can go home to your wife and quit your mopin' after a God that would turn you oot if you fell on 'ard times. You can count your blessins' you 'ave a livin', breathin' person to go home to. You can pretend you doon't know me if we ever meet again."

Race left. He went as far as the saloon and stayed in the shadows where he could watch the alley. When Aoife left, he followed at a distance, determined to see her home safely whether she welcomed it or not. He would have done it the first night he'd me her if he'd had his wits about him. There were far too many drunk and rowdy cowboys on this side of town.

He followed her across the tracks and watched her go in a side door of the social club. *Hard times, indeed.* She didn't look like any whore he'd ever seen before. This time of night, she should have been working to earn her keep. He hoped for her sake she had another job at the club. At least this explained the priest's behavior. He didn't agree with it, but he wasn't surprised.

He took out his pocket watch and angled it toward the moonlight so he could read the face. *Late enough.* He hated avoiding Millie, hated hurting her feelings. He told himself repeatedly it was the best course of action to avoid bigger hurt in the future. His stomach grumbled. Time to head home to his cold dinner and colder bed.

****

Millie closed the book and fanned her face. Her body certainly responded to those fiction words written by a man. She couldn't imagine any woman behaving like Fanny Hill. Did men want women to behave that way? Whores maybe, but not wives. Granted, maybe if wives acted like that sometimes, husbands wouldn't patronize brothels.

She would finish her dress, ask Sarah to help her with her make-up, and pretend she had the boldness of Una. Depending on how Race reacted, if it didn't work, she'd resort to some of Fanny's tactics.

Race's tread sounded on the stairs and the apartment door opened then closed softly. She caught her breath and heat burned low in her pelvis. Her body urged her to rush out to the kitchen and confront her husband right then. Taking a deep breath, she calmed herself, leaned over, and turned out the lamp. She had a solid plan now. Moving too fast would only jeopardize it. She needed to think of Race as a cornered chicken. He would look for a way to slip away from her until she was so close, he sat down in the corner and gave up. She probably shouldn't think of her husband as a chicken but it did cool her heated body enough so she could sleep.

****

Race strained to get his wrench in the correct position.

"Can it go any higher?" Alfred asked for the third time.

"No." Race grunted as he tightened the bolts holding the ostentatious clock to the eight-inch beam. "If we stack more wood on to make it higher it will be unstable and more apt to fall."

"Yes, yes, right. Can't afford a lawsuit," the banker mumbled.

"Father, it is the grandest thing in the entire town. It doesn't need to be higher for folks to notice it." Fredrick stood next to Race on a second ladder holding the clock steady.

"You're correct, of course, my boy. Now we look like a respectable business, not a shanty for miners to store their gold."

Race gave the clock a jerk. Satisfied it was secure,

he climbed down. Fredrick followed and collected both ladders to store. Race checked all three faces with his own pocket watch and turned to the senior Mountroy. "Installation was included with your purchase, so it looks like our business is concluded."

Alfred turned from admiring the timepiece and clapped Race on the back. "That it is. Thank you. You've been very accommodating having to wait on the build for so long. Your own business is doing well, I understand."

"Yes. I've had a steady stream of folks needing repairs and Millie has been busy with orders and mending as well. I think she'll like living in Wylder."

"Very good. I enjoy seeing commerce expand. Come inside, I have something for you."

Race followed the man inside the original bank. The new one's interior wasn't quite finished.

Alfred presented Race with a bottle of scotch whisky. "This is an excellent year from my private collection. Please accept it as a token of my thanks and esteem."

Race eyed the bottle as if it were a snake but reluctantly took it. It was excellent, his favorite imported brand. "Thank you, sir. It was my pleasure. Good luck finishing your build."

"Great things are coming. I feel it." Alfred smiled.

Chapter 9

Race shouldn't be in bed at six o'clock in the evening, leaving Millie alone to close up the shop. Skipping lunch had been a mistake and he certainly shouldn't attempt to soak the rest of his problems in the other half bottle of the fine scotch he held in his hand.

The sun streaming through his bedroom window caught the glass bottle and sent little rainbows across the wall. The liquid inside looked like honey. He should write that down. He'd never before considered being a poet but thought he might be quite good.

Now, back to his problems. He could write those down and cross them off as he drownded each one. Drone…drowd, drownd? Cross them off as he eliminated each one.

One, he lusted for his wife daily. He admitted that out loud in his head because he was a little tipsy. Two, his wife was a beautiful, volutuosness, volomuess, voluptumous… finely formed woman and not at all his sister.

Wait. Which one of those was the problem? Her prettiness or that she wasn't his sister? Four, no, five, his visits to the churches didn't revolve around Rosemary and Mary Catherine anymore, only his troubles with Millie.

Six, no one agreed he was doing the right thing by freeing Millie of himself. So, why do it? Oh, right, he was a bad, broken, besotted, burly, bosom... Race laughed. Where was he going with that? It didn't matter. He had ten problems and the eleventh was his half-empty bottle of excellent scotch. So beautiful, the color of honey, he poured another glass and toasted the empty room. "To my problems. May they go for a swim in a bottle of gin!" That was quite good. He should write it down.

****

Millie followed her last customer to the door and turned the sign to 'closed'. It might be easier to make new garments rather than sew patches on patches of the threadbare pile he'd left. Bachelors were funny that way, she'd found.

She turned to Sarah and Una who were still there visiting. Millie had been working up her nerve all afternoon to ask them for assistance with her plan. They would leave soon; she couldn't put it off any longer. "Before you go, I need to ask you both something."

"The answer is yes, Amos really is more of a gossip than a little old lady," Una said, and Sarah nodded in agreement, referring the man who'd just left.

Millie laughed. "You might have told me he was talking about his mule instead of a wife before I suggested a new dress might make her feel better." The man went on and on about Stella. Of course, Millie thought he'd been talking about a wife. Though she did think it odd he would share about his wife being frisky in the mornings. "Actually, I have a favor to ask."

"Don't look so terrified. Nothing could be so bad." Sarah patted Caleb's back. The six-year-old had come with her that afternoon and completely wore himself, and his mother out with playing and making mischief.

He now slept sprawled across Sarah's lap. She said she didn't mind because he rarely held still for her to hold him anymore.

Millie concocted a story to tell her new friends so she wouldn't have to explain her true marital situation. "Race and I have been so busy traveling and opening the shop, our marriage has, ah, gotten a little routine. I want to surprise him. I'm looking for some tips."

Una appraised Millie's work dress. "I'd start with something a little less drab."

"Oh! I've taken care of that. Let me show you." She went to a shelf and pulled off a bundle wrapped in muslin. She set it on the table and unwrapped her finished garnet dress.

Una approached and fingered the trim. "This is lovely. The color is perfect. I own something similar."

Millie blushed. "Yes. I based the pattern after the dress you wore last week."

"Hold it up, let me see," Sarah called from her seat.

Una did so.

"I love it! You do such beautiful work. I can't believe you made it from just looking at Una's dress."

Millie shrugged. "I've made so many dresses for myself, it goes quickly. Many parts are basically the same."

"What else do you need help with?" Sarah asked.

Her face burned. "Well, what to say. What to do. I read a book—"

"Oh, have you, now?" Una laughed. "What kind of book?"

"Fanny Hill," Millie whispered.

"I've not read that," Sarah said from her chair.

Una tapped her chin. "Hmm. That's a good one.

Probably a little advanced in technique than what you're looking for."

"I only had one beau before Rick." Sarah absently ran her fingers through Caleb's hair as he slept on. "We burned hot but didn't last. I went straight from Russ to marrying Rick. I knew he was the one for me. We experienced a lull after I gave birth. I wanted to resume marital relations, but Rick treated me like fragile glass. I finally had to order him to bed."

"That's a good method," Una agreed. "The dress will help."

"I have cosmetics, too. Race never let me wear it. I have to hide it in my r—in my trunk. I don't have any experience putting it on."

"You need a light touch, otherwise you look like a whore. Some men go for that, though." Una looked at Millie who shook her head. Una shrugged. "I can help you put it on so you can barely tell it's there, but it will enhance your natural attributes."

"Go put your dress on," Sarah said. "We'll talk over other ideas while Una does your face."

****

1848

"Dang it!" Millie cursed as she wiped away the eye powder from her left eye for the third time. She reached for her hair in frustration, a habit Bethy had been trying to break her of, forgetting she'd put it up off her neck. She thought it made her look older, except for the combs that kept wantin' to come out. She found a loose strand at her nape and yanked it out.

"You can do this, Mildred," she said to herself. "Flushed mad cheeks are not going to win you a husband. Just make ya look like a crybaby." She

stretched out her cramped fingers and tried again. This time getting a smooth pink streak on her left lid that nearly matched the right. She wiped the powder off her finger and picked up the jar of red crème. She took a dab on each middle finger and worked it in small circles on each cheek. Satisfied, she put another dab on her index finger and traced her lips. Too thin. She'd always admired Bethesda's full, pouty lips and the men seemed to like them too. She traced her original line then puckered at her mirror. Better.

****

"Lord, Millie. You're blushing like a virgin. I'm not even gonna use rouge on you," Una said as she traced a fine coal line on Millie's eyelid.

"The dress already gives her some color. I agree, no rouge is needed," Sarah added.

"Ah oo I ay?" Millie asked while trying to hold her face perfectly still for Una.

"Say? Just bat your eyelashes and give him an inviting look. That should do it." Sarah was still giving advice from her chair since Caleb was dead to the world.

"I've always enjoyed a little pretend play." Una finished Millie's face and began fussing with her hair. "We want this to look gently tousled, like you just came from a lover's bed."

"What do you mean 'pretend play'?

"Acting like different people. My favorite lately has been 'carpenter and homeowner'. Mmm." Una closed her eyes. "Oh, yes, please, sir, hammer those shingles. You're soo sweaty. Why don't you take your shirt off? Where are you going to drive that long, stiff fence picket?"

"Una!" Sarah exclaimed.

Millie put her hand to her lips to cover her surprise. She'd met Ambrose Barlow in town and couldn't picture him any of those scenarios. Ew. Race, on the other hand, didn't remove his shirt in her presence often, but when he did… Let's just say the last thing she pictured him doing was repairing a roof.

"Well, you get the idea," Una said. She combed out hunks of hair, curled them softly around her hand and laid them gently on Millie's shoulders. "Tell Race he needs to wind you up. He's a clock man."

"Or you want to swing on his pendulum." Sarah laughed shrilly, waking Caleb.

"See what makes him tick!" Una said.

"Grind his gears?" Millie suggested, beginning to understand the game.

Both women exploded in renewed peals of mirth.

"You've got it. I need to go meet Rick. I'm running behind already, but he'd probably chewing the fat with Ralph Wylder and hasn't noticed. She helped a groggy Caleb off her lap and took him by the hand. "Do tell me how it goes next week."

They said good-bye and Una put the final touches on Millie's hair. "I'm not gonna wait till next week. I'll be by sooner." With a wink, Una followed Sarah and Caleb out the door.

Millie took a breath as deep as her corset would allow. She felt like her breasts were almost up around her chin, but Una approved the affect. She re-locked the front door and pulled the curtains closed. Dusk settled in as she climbed the stairs to their home. She'd been so nervous all day, she'd not given a thought to dinner. Race went up earlier, after finishing at the bank. She wasn't hungry, but she hoped he'd made dinner for himself, at least.

He wasn't sitting at the dining table as she'd expected, nor did she find him reading in his chair. After a brief search of the other rooms, the only place left was Race's bedroom. No light shown from under the door. Had he already turned in? Was he ill?

She should forget her whole plan. It would never work if Race was sick. No. She wouldn't scrap it before even walking through the door. She would be bold. She touched the cool knob and paused to listen. She heard a masculine chuckle. Reading in the dark, surely not? She turned the knob. "Race?"

She'd placed her lamp on the hall table. Its light shone faintly into the room, illuminating familiar furniture and her husband's form on the bed. "Race, are you all right?"

"Right as rain, Mills, darlin."

She ventured further into the room. "You don't sound yourself."

"I'm not nobody else, much as I'd like to be."

Millie could now make out the glass in his hand and three-quarters empty bottle on the nightstand. "Why would you like to be somebody else, Race?"

"Cause then I wouldn't have ten-ty-five problems." He snickered.

He was completely soused! She'd never known Race to drink more than a glass or two of liquor. "Race, what problems do you have? What can I do to help?" This was serious, and much more important than her silly plan. Her husband needed her.

"You! You're fifty of my problems. Standing there all delable, decatable, delatable. Damn! Pretty!

Standing there so pretty. What am I supposed to do? How am I supposed to protect you? I can't even remember what I'm protecting you from, dammit."

Millie tried to make sense of his ramblings. Race called her pretty, after he tried to call her delectable. Now drink made him forget why he wouldn't touch her. She smiled. Her plan was back on. Her palms turned clammy. She wiped them on her skirt and stepped up to the bed. The door was still open, and from this vantage she no longer blocked the light and Race could see her dress.

"You shouldn't have glass in the bed, Race. You could cut yourself." She bent over him to retrieve the tumbler from his hand. She reached across his body and angled her cleavage, so it passed practically under his nose. She heard him take a sharp breath in.

"Mills," he moaned.

She straightened and placed it on the table next to the bottle. She wondered momentarily if this would be considered taking advantage but decided she didn't much care. That was being bold.

"Are you going to sleep in your suit? It looks uncomfortable. Let me help you." Millie sat down on the edge of the bed, her hip touching his. She reached for his tie. It was already loose, so she finished the job and slowly pulled it from his neck. "This vest is also very constricting." She began working the buttons.

Race lay very still. He watched her fingers for a minute, then reached up and traced her cheek with a finger. "So soft." It continued down and brushed the exposed portion of her breasts.

Millie shivered. The same heat as when she read about Fanny Hill, again pooled in her core. "Race," she whispered. "Sit up so I can help you take this off." She leaned back to give him space.

Race sat up. Millie moved to help him with his clothes, but instead he pulled her forward with his hand cradling her head. He mashed his lips to hers like a brand. He moaned her name as he dragged his lips to her neck. Meanwhile, his other hand kneaded her thigh, urging her closer still.

Millie barely registered his whiskey-tainted breath. All her Fanny Hill and Una lessons escaped her, and she tumbled along like a leaf in a brook. All the feelings she'd read about were magnified a hundred times. The man she loved really wanted her! She turned her head to kiss whatever she could reach. Mostly hair, but Race didn't seem to mind. His tongue delved down the front of her dress. She moaned. "Race, yes!"

Apparently all the affirmation he needed, he flipped her to her back and straddled one of her thighs. This position caused her breasts to heave and nearly breach her bodice. Race noticed and immediately aided their escape. If Millie hadn't sewn them on so securely, her mother of pearl buttons would have gone flying. His warm fingers grazed the skin of her breast, then lifted it away from its confines. He replaced his hand with his mouth. The sensation of his warm mouth and gentle suction on her nipple almost sent Millie through the ceiling.

He gave her other breast equal attention, and when she thought she could take no more, Race shifted to straddle both of her legs. Yards of garnet fabric bunched between them and something hard pressed into the apex of her thighs. He pressed again and she raised her hips to meet him. She moved her hands to his waist and pulled him into her again. He ground down again while moving his lips back to her neck and mouth. The cool air on her damp nipples added to the sensations between her legs. Her body reached for something, but for what, she didn't know, only that Race could take her there. She badly wanted to spread her legs, but she was pinned. She panted and moaned Race's name. He put his hand beneath her and pressed her into him. Something was happening. He released her backside and took her nipple between two fingers and squeezed while surging into her again.

Millie's world exploded. She forgot to breathe as powerful ripples cascaded through her, emanating from her core. Race growled and wrenched her bodice down. A sharp ripping rent the air. He stilled. He was off of her in a second.

"Millie. Oh, no. Dammit. I'm sorry." He backed away, stumbling into the doorframe. "I'm sorry." He turned and disappeared. Second later the outside door slammed.

She'd just had the best experience of her life and her husband ran from her. Well, he wasn't getting away that easily. She sat up and swung her legs to the floor.

Chapter 10

Race staggered past the Five Star Saloon. He had to get to the church. He'd done the exact thing he'd been trying to avoid. Damnable drink! It wasn't right to blame the alcohol. It only lowered his resistance. What occurred had been brewing in Race's blood for a while. Every moan, every breath, every damn time she said his name, it was like his dreams made real. He tripped over legs in his path and got a face full of dirt.

"Watch it, yous!" slurred a cowboy sitting on the ground against the saloon.

That's probably what he looked like to Millie when he attacked her. He pushed to his knees, only to fall back on his hind end. A delicate hand appeared in front of his face.

"Be off with you, clock man, you don't belong 'ere." Aoife McCarthy stood over him.

Even in his drunken state, he saw the buzzards begin to circle. "Neither do you. Git and leave me be."

"Wouldn't be very good repayment for you seein' me 'ome safe de other night, now would it?" She grabbed his arm and yanked. He had no choice but to move with her or drag her down with him.

"You need a fella you don't have to carry, sweet thing?" A stocky man approached from the saloon.

Race was in no position to defend anyone's honor. Best to diffuse the situation rather than get into a pissing match. "Little woman's just seeing me home." He wrapped an arm around Aoife's waist. She stiffened and he prayed she wouldn't smack him.

"That so? You'd best get her tucked away before someone bigger takes her offa yer hands." The man narrowed his eyes, as if looking for a crack in Race's story.

"Aim to. Let's go, darling." Race forced himself not to stagger. He stared down two other men as he and Aoife made their way back to Sidewinder Lane.

As soon as they left the light of the saloon behind, Aoife did hit him. She wrenched her body away from his but returned her arm to his waist when he swayed. The entire way back she kept up a steady litany of creative ways to describe what a fool he was, all with an Irish lilt. He imagined she was Rosemary, risen from the dead, to berate him.

When they reached his store, Race let himself into the shop rather than go upstairs to face his wife. He'd sleep on the floor of his workroom. It was no better than he deserved.

"How will you get home?" he asked Aoife as she untangled herself from him.

"Buckboard Alley is quiet this time o' night. I'll stay to de shadows and be just fine. I doon't know what is wrong with you tonight, but you need a keeper. I've no intention o' takin on de job, so I'll tell you dis only once. No mahr, Mr. Lowery. No mahr goin to de church. If God be there, 'es not goin to solve your problem." She peered at him solemnly in the darkness.

"How will you stop me?"

"I don't know as yet. You seem like a good man. I 'ad a good man, and I would give anythin' to 'ave 'im back. Go on an' be a good man to your wife, Mr. Lowery."

"But I'm not."

"Frum what I be seein', she's got mahr faith in you than you've got in yourself. Let her 'eal what ails you an' leave God alone." Aoife stepped off the porch and disappeared into the darkness.

Race locked the door and went to do a night of penance on the floor of his workroom.

****

Millie stood outside the shop door and contemplated confronting Race while her anger was fresh. He was still drunk. She shouldn't assume the worst of him when Aoife may well have been the one taking advantage. Not a whore? That was a load of balderdash. What was Aoife McCarthy doing with her dirty papist arm around Millie's husband? She never had a thing against Catholics before other than Race's late wife had been one and gave him all kinds of ideas about sin and repentance. If that Aoife was looking to better her situation, she was looking in the wrong place.

And Race! He was far too familiar with the woman he'd only briefly met twice. Tears threatened. Did he see Aoife every time he went to the church or out walking?

She waited in the shadows until she saw Aoife exit the shop. The woman slipped between the buildings and headed in the direction of the social club.

Millie couldn't decide if her encounter with Race earlier that evening improved their marital relationship or made things worse. Only time would tell.

Being a shrew wouldn't endear her husband to her. She'd go to the social club the next day and confront

Aoife as well as charge Adelaide to keep her employees on their own side of the tracks. Their business was to service the men who sought them out, not solicit husbands in town. She turned and headed up the stairs to her bed. If Race wanted to sleep on the floor rather than in her bed, she'd let him. But not for much longer.

****

1838

Millie awoke to a soft kiss on her cheek. She peered into the darkness, sensing her mother nearby. "Mama?"

"Sweet, Millie. I couldn't leave without saying good-bye," her mother whispered.

"Where you goin?" Dark was for sleeping, not leaving.

"Oh, honey, I have to go away."

Millie squirmed to get out of bed, but her mother was sitting on her blanket, pinning her in. "I go, too."

"No, sweet girl. You must stay here." Her voice sounded funny. "And take care of Papa."

"When will you come back?"

"I don't know, but I'll try to come for you real soon." Her mother rubbed Millie's back now, like she did before bedtime.

Despite her sleepiness, Millie's eyes filled with tears. "Don't go, Mama."

"Sh, sh. I must. Bethy will help you. You go to her if you need anything. You hear?" Continuing to rub her back, her mother stood. Then she tucked the blanket around her and kissed her cheek again. "Stay in bed, young lady. If you get out, you'll get whippings from Papa." Mama was stern now.

"Nooo!" Millie whined into her mattress. Tears

flowed now.

"I love you, always, Mildred. Be a good girl."

"Mama, no," Millie moaned. She wanted to jump out of bed and follow her mother, but she feared the idea of a whipping. At four years old, she'd never received one, but she's seen Papa use the whip on the horse. She'd wait and follow so her mother wouldn't hear her. She lay still in her bed pretending to sleep, counting as high as she could over and over, waiting for the right moment to sneak away. 1, 2, 3, 4, 5. She wouldn't fall asleep for real. 1, 2, 3, 4, 5. 1, 2, 3...4, 5. 1...2, 3...4...1...2...

****

Early the next morning, Millie rapped sharply on the door of the social club. After several moments with no answer, she rapped again. The residents kept late hours, but someone should be up. Putting her ear to the door, she tried to detect sound from within. Anything she might have heard was drowned out by the train pulling up to the platform down the road a piece. She shifted her basket to her left arm and tried the knob. To her surprise, the door opened. She'd find Mrs. Willowby herself.

As she made her way down the hallway that led to the madam's receiving room, a commotion came from behind one of the closed doors. She could identify Adelaide's voice and Aoife's lilt, as well as that of a hysterical woman. None of her business. She'd wait in Adelaide's room.

She found the door to the room where they'd had tea last time. It was wide open, so Millie didn't truly feel like she was invading the woman's privacy. Though she hadn't particularly noticed Addie's scent when she last visited, a light floral aroma lingered throughout the space. She pulled the borrowed book from her basket and moved to the bookshelf. It surprised her to see a second volume and considered asking to borrow it as well. In light of the pointed conversation she intended to have with the owner, she didn't think she'd continue to be allowed lending privileges.

She placed the first volume next to the second and went to sit. On the table next to Adelaide's chair sat an interrupted breakfast and a letter. Next to it lay a childishly drawn picture of what appeared to be a dog, or perhaps a mouse. She leaned closer to get a better look.

At the bottom of the page, a series of lines and circles imitated words. After the scribble were very adult letters that read, 'To Mother'. Adelaide? A mother? Where was her child? Obviously, not in Wylder if she was receiving mail from her.

Giving in to her curiosity, she turned the letter so she could see the words.

Adelaide,

As you can see, Eliza Jane has been working on her letters. She wants to be able to write you herself as she doesn't believe I entreat you to come for her in every letter on her behalf. She's a clever child and will eventually see through your thin excuses. I appreciate the money you send for her care, but it breaks my heart to hear her pray every night that you and 'Papa Farley' will set up your household quickly so she can finally join you. But I repeat myself.

I'm thankful for your continued desire to hear about your daughter as it gives me the opportunity to express my frustration with this untenable situation. Mr. Standish disappeared in the wind when I continued to be unable to tell him how long I'd be responsible for my niece. He was a good man and my best prospect thus far. I fear spinsterhood is my future.

I am angry, but I also fear for you. I told you Farley Willowby stunk of untruth. Now, he has taken you away from your only family with no good reason, or none you will divulge. I continue to pray for your safety. I'm relieved every time I receive post from Wylder—

"What are you doing here?"

Millie whipped her hand back as if stung, too surprised and embarrassed to speak.

"Well? Who let you in?" Adelaide demanded, stalking to her seat. A fresh floral wave replaced the lingering scent as she passed.

She didn't mention the letter, so maybe she didn't see Millie reading it. Inwardly sighing in relief, she forged ahead with her original intent. "For one, I was returning your book. I replaced it on the shelf. It was very informative, thank you."

"If there is one, there must be a two." Adelaide took a bite of her toast and wrinkled her nose.

"Yes, well, I'd appreciate it if you'd keep your girls away from my husband." She tilted her nose in the air.

Adelaide stared at Millie. She picked up her tea and took a swallow, grimacing before replacing it on the saucer. "I don't make a habit of turning men away from the club. It's bad for business. If you can't keep your husband at home, it seems the book you borrowed wasn't very helpful after all."

Millie tried not to let the barb catch hold. "My husband did not come here. One of your girls threw herself at him in town last night."

"Which girl? And if you know this happened, why didn't you stop it yourself?" She leaned back in her seat but still held Millie's eyes.

"I saw Aoife with Race last night and have reason to believe this was not the first such occasion." She clenched her fists in her lap. She hated confrontation.

A condescending smile stretched across the woman's face. "Aoife!!" she yelled.

Millie jumped and spun to the door.

A harried Aoife appeared with a damp towel in her hand. "What do you need? I've got me 'ands full with calmin' Amber right now, don't I?"

"I apologize for taking you from your work. I just have a question. Did you go to town last night for the purpose of enticing Mr. Lowery with your feminine wiles?"

Aoife turned to Millie and snorted. "Not likely. I'm still mournin' me own. I've no interest in takin on your man an 'is ridiculous notions. I've got things to do." She turned on her heel and went, presumably, back to Amber.

"There. Now if there's nothing else you need." Adelaide began to rise.

"Where's your child?" Millie blurted out. Now that she'd gotten another good look at Aoife, she doubted her assumption about her designs on Race. That, and the woman's complete absence of artifice, convinced her. She needed to fix her own problems with her husband and not spend time battling windmills. Now, the question of Adelaide's daughter nagged her for an answer.

Adelaide froze, then sank back into her seat. "You looked at my private correspondence. I don't need to dignify your question with an answer." She reached for her tea, hesitated then returned her hand to her lap.

"Please. You have a child, don't you? Where is she?" Millie couldn't hide the pleading in her voice.

"Why? So, you can be critical of my decisions? I thought we were forming a friendship, Mildred. You've barged into my home, invaded my privacy, and now asked questions that are none of your business. Because of your past, you didn't judge us. Why is knowing about my daughter so important to you?"

"So, I can understand. Where is she?"

Adelaide sighed. "She's lives back east with my sister. She is well cared for, and I visit as often as I can."

"But how could you leave her?" She wiped at a tear.

"After her father died, I remarried. I planned to bring her here after we set up our household." She stood and walked to the window. She kept her back to Millie as she continued. "I found myself in a situation I could not escape. I was in a strange land at the complete mercy of my new husband, who turned out to not be what he presented himself to be. I cannot bring my daughter here. Surely you understand."

In the silence, Millie watched as a dust mote caught the sunlight and floated to the ground. She waited till the other woman finally turned and met her gaze. "When I have a child, nothing will separate me from her. Nothing."

Adelaide's response was equally stony. "I truly

hope you are able to keep that promise. Eliza Jane is well provided for. She will have an excellent education."

"But she won't have you," Millie whispered.

Adelaide's gaze softened and her eyes grew moist. "I send money for her care. If I leave, I will have nothing. I won't have the means to support her or myself. I am stuck here and am making the best of the situation. I have five girls who need me to advocate for them and protect them. I have learned to be satisfied with that, if not happy."

"But how could you leave her?" Millie's tears flowed freely now.

"Millie, I am not like your mother. I can only explain my reasons and that I did not intend to be separated from her permanently. It pains me every single day, but I've learned to set it aside and continue on. I cannot speak for your mother's reasons. And I am done speaking on the subject. You need to go home to your husband and your shop. Please don't contact me again until you have a dress ready."

Millie wiped her tears away one last time and stood. "I'll not darken your door again. I'll get word to you and you can send a girl to pick up the dress. I beg you, please consider your daughter and what your absence is doing to her."

"I do consider my daughter. Every single day. Stop comparing my situation to your history. I know what's best for Eliza Jane. I hope this unpleasant morning won't hurt our business arrangement." Adelaide rose and escorted her to the door.

Millie stiffened her spine. "I too, have to make a living. Lowery's Frocks and Clocks will not turn business away for personal reasons. Good day, madam."

Chapter 11

Race had never experienced a pounding in his head so insistent. It clamored both inside and outside his skull. Of course, it had been at least six years since he'd drank so much. It felt like morning, but he loathed the thought of opening his eyes to confirm it. If only that dad-blame pounding would stop, he could get his bearings and figure out what to do about things he could remember from the night before.

Opting to keep his eyes closed, he rolled over to his stomach and rose to his hands and knees. He realized the drumming in his head had a different rhythm to that outside.

"Mister Low-rie! Mister Low-rie, you in there?" A child's voice came from the front of the shop.

What time was it? Where was Millie? Who had a clock emergency at this time of morning? He sighed. Alfred would have a clock emergency at this time of morning. He needed to open his eyes. He did so, then immediately squinted. It was later than he thought. He swayed. No standing yet, then. He crawled to Millie's worktable so he could assist himself to his feet.

The knocking persisted. "Mister Low-rie!"

Race dragged his feet to the door, unlatched it, and yanked it open. "What!"

A boy of about eight stood on the stoop. "Mister Smithers sent me to fetch ya. Says to tell ya the preacher's in town but not for long."

Race dug a half-cent piece out of his pocket and handed it to the boy. "Thanks, kid."

The boy took off and Race re-locked the door. In light of what he'd done last night, a visit to the preacher was well in order.

The church was empty, so Race went to the rectory looking for the preacher. Through the open door, Race could see Mrs. Smithers at the stove. Robert Smithers sat at the table drinking coffee with a man who's back faced the entrance. The smell of bacon made his stomach roll but at least the pounding in his head had diminished.

He knocked on the doorframe to announce himself. Robert motioned for him to come in and the other man turned. The man's full beard couldn't disguise his familiar face.

"Rocky Jameson, I should have guessed." A smile split Race's face.

The man cleared his throat and the tops of his cheeks pinkened. "I go by Rochester Jameson now, but, ah, usually just Preacher James. Race Lowery, or do you go by Horace, now?"

Race laughed and stepped into the house to embrace his old friend. "I never go by Horace if I can help it."

Robert rose and shook Race's hand then invited him to sit. "Sal, fix another plate for Race."

"Oh no, no thank you. I could do with a coffee if you've got some to spare, though." Race settled into a chair. The excitement caused his head to start pounding anew.

Robert retrieved another cup from the cabinet and

filled it from the pot on the stove.

"This is the man who was desperate to see me?" Rocky raised his bushy eyebrows at Robert.

"Quite so. I take it you're familiar." Robert placed a steaming mug in front of Race.

"We were roommates my first year at seminary. How long's it been, Race?"

Race took a hearty swallow of coffee, willing the cobwebs to dissipate. "Over a dozen years."

Rocky sobered. "I was right sorry to hear about Rosemary and your little girl. I'd hoped you'd come back and pick up where you left off."

"There was no going back."

Mrs. Smithers set plates in front of Robert and the preacher.

"Sal, it's a beautiful morning. Let's break our fast outside."

She started to protest, but glanced at Rocky and instead, followed her husband out the door.

"Tell me." Rocky's gaze rested on Race as he stuffed a forkful of eggs in his mouth.

Race told him of his grief and his difficulties with his faith. He shared the circumstances which led to his ill-advised marriage.

Rocky's look of concern turned to amusement when Race began explaining his current predicament. "What is it, exactly, that you need from me?"

"An annulment."

Rocky's eyes lit up and he rocked back in his chair with a bark of laughter. Race didn't join him. "Seriously? Whatever for? God has granted you a second chance at happiness. Why would you throw away such a blessing?"

"It's a blessing I don't deserve, and what of Millie's happiness?"

Rocky smiled again. "From what you've told me, it sounds like having a real marriage would bring you both happiness."

Race scowled into his coffee cup. "She's too young to know any better. She'd regret having me before long. Can you grant us an annulment or not?"

Rocky sighed. "We covered it the last year of seminary, so let me remember the rules. We don't like to grant them, especially in this part of the country. Marriage is serious business and being a woman alone in the west has different concerns than it does in the east."

"I'll see her well taken care of. You know I won't let harm come to her."

The preacher gave him a skeptical look. "She wasn't of marriageable age, but she did have parental consent, correct?"

Race nodded.

Rocky ticked off the item by holding up one finger. "Authorized celebrant?"

"He appeared to be a real preacher, yes."

Another finger went up. "You're not kin." A third finger joined the first two. "Adultery by either party?"

"Of course not. You know I'm an honorable man." Race was losing patience with the list.

Rocky held up four fingers now. "Last question. Is she barren?"

Race launched himself from his seat. "How would I know? I told you we've been living as siblings."

"For six years? Do all your parts work?" He smirked.

"My parts work fine," Race growled.

"That's it then. I can't grant an annulment, there's no grounds." He dug back into his breakfast with a satisfied grin.

"But we haven't consummated the union." Race ran a hand through his hair.

"That's a myth. If you'd come back to seminary, you'd know it, and you would have avoided your present situation. Looks like you were saving your virtue for nothing, Horace."

Race sat back down and returned to his coffee, wishing for something stronger.

"I wish I could meet this girl who has you so tied up in knots. Your problems are all in your head. If you think you need forgiveness, you're wrong. You've already received it. Only thing wrong now is that you're not participating fully in a God-blessed union. You need to rectify that straight away. But the only way to end your marriage is divorce." He gave Race a hard look. "And that would be a sin and a shame."

"I'll think on it. Why don't you come by the shop and meet her?"

"I'll try, but I've got a sermon to preach this morning. Then I've got to pack up my things from here, make my rounds, and get ready to catch the stage on Tuesday."

"I meant to ask what brought you back to town so soon. Robert didn't expect you for a month."

"Telegraph caught up to me about a week back. My mother's ailing and I need to take a leave of absence. I'm leaving from here cause I wouldn't trust Magdalene with anyone but Chet Daniels for that length of time. She's too set in her ways to be happy in

Boston."

"The filly you got before I left? Unbelievable."

"What can I say? Some things are worth hanging on to."

Chapter 12

1838

Dearest Beth,
I hope this letter finds you and Millie well. Thank you for watching over her; I think about her every day. I often wondered if I made the right decision. As hard as it was and still is, I can now say 'yes'. I have a new daughter! We've named her Winnifred. She has the same gray eyes as Millie, and I can already tell her hair will be as thick and wavy. She is a beauty and Philip is as in love with her as I am. Please continue to write me about Millie's life. If you feel she's ever in danger from Otis, please tell me. I'll convince Philip to bring her to live with us.
I'll let you decide what you want to tell her about me. You must think me a terrible mother and friend to saddle you with this responsibility, but I hope you remember me kindly to Millie. Please explain to her how it was, how Otis was. You know. You saw.
You are a better friend than I deserve.
Annie Chambers

****

Millie trudged home, not caring who saw her crossing the tracks. There were only a few places on the south side of town open on Sunday morning, and none of them respectable. She found it laughable that folks might question her presence at the Social Club; her, the least-bedded woman in town.

She mulled over her argument with Addie. Though she lamented the loss of a possible friend and ally, she couldn't overlook abandonment. She knew exactly how little Eliza Jane felt; she'd lived it herself. She'd never be able to look at Adelaide again without thinking about the childishly draw picture of a dog-mouse. A tear slipped down her cheek, and she swiped it away.

She was glad to not have to open the shop. Attending Sunday morning worship would probably be a good thing for her and Race to do, but until he worked out the demons haunting him, it was out of the question.

Two men staggered out of the Five Star, or perhaps the entertaining rooms above stairs, and turned up Sidewinder Lane, her destination. She slowed her pace so she wouldn't overtake them. They stopped outside the dress shop to talk to a woman waiting on the stoop. What could she want? Not even the saloons were open on Sunday mornings.

"Ah sweetie, I've got some time to spare to show ya around town. Come on."

"No, thank you. I'm meeting someone," the woman responded primly, though her eyes darted nervously. They lit on Millie. "And here she is."

Millie approached her shop. "Get along gentlemen, or do I need to call my husband down?"

Then men grumbled but continued on their way. Millie assessed her guest. The woman, girl more accurately wore a desperately wilted, stylish pink dress. The matching hat drooped where the brim bent irreparably. She sat on a small valise, her elbow propped on her knees and chin resting on her palms.

She stood as Millie approached.

"Are you Mildred Lowery?" the girl asked, wary.

"I am. We're closed this morning and I have a number of things to attend to. You'll have to return in the morning." She made to bypass the shop and go upstairs.

"Wait, you don't understand." The girl caught Millie's basket.

Millie waited for the girl to continue. There wasn't much she could do for her besides sewing or giving her a meal, though rumpled, she didn't appear destitute.

The girl stood and brushed off her skirts. "I came to see you. I'm your sister, Winnie."

Millie took a step back. This time when she looked at the girl, she paid attention to more than just her clothes. Her thick, blonde hair was pulled back and fastened at the nape of her neck. Thousands of tendrils had escaped during her journey, but what remained in the clip was full and wavey like Millie's own. Her eyes were the same gray she saw in her own mirror. The girl's lips were uniquely her own, but her general face shape reminded Millie of her mother.

"Why are you here?" Millie didn't mean to snap, but really, why was she here? She couldn't be more than sixteen. Old enough to be married, but not to travel all the way from Savannah alone.

Tears welled up in Winnie's eyes and spilled down her cheeks. "Mother's gone."

Millie had been expecting the news, though not the personal delivery. She searched her soul and found no sorrow there. "I'm sorry for your loss."

"Our loss," Winnie sobbed.

"She was your mother much longer than she was

mine. I barely remember her." She found she mourned the loss of the relationship more than the actual woman.

"She talked about you always. I lived in your shadow my whole life. I never had our mother's whole heart." She dug a hanky out of her sleeve and wiped her nose.

"I never had any of her heart, nor did I have her in body. You certainly got the better of it." It was no use taking her frustration out on this pathetic creature. "Come. This isn't a conversation for the street."

Millie led Winnie up the stairs and showed her where she could wash. She took cups out of the cabinet and heated water for tea.

"Can I change?" Winnie called from the washroom. "I've been wearing this dress for days."

Millie sighed. Once Winnie closed herself in smaller bedroom, Millie poured the heated water into a basin. She added a little cold water, soap and a cloth and brought them to her sister. "Pass me your dress and petticoat so I can hang them to air out." Winnie handed her not one, but three petticoats and a very travel-worn dress. Bundling them in her arms, she went to the door, They'd be fresh as anything on such a pretty day. She shifted her burden to reach for the knob, only to have it opened by her wayward husband.

"Millie, we need to talk."

"We do," she agreed. "But not right now; we have a house guest. Be a dear and entertain my sister while I hang these out." She eased past him and headed down the stairs.

Race turned and followed her. "What do you mean 'your sister'? Doesn't she live with your mother in Savannah?"

Millie draped the first petticoat over the rope line and secured it with a wooden pin. "I suppose she may reside in Savannah with her father, but my mother died recently. Winnie came to tell me." She threw the petticoat over.

"Ah, Mills. I'm sorry." Race pulled Millie into an embrace, laundry and all.

She accepted the hug stiffly. Her emotions were all tumbled up inside her. She should feel more sadness about her mother's passing, but just couldn't. There was still too much hurt. Now, here in Race's arms, the place she'd been vying to be for weeks, she couldn't bring herself to enjoy it. It was comforting, brotherly, the same way he'd embraced her dozens of times before. Of course, he was trying to comfort her in her sorrow. It shouldn't feel like a romantic hug. Tumultuous. That was the word for her emotions. She wanted scream at Winnie and Race and lock herself in her room until... her room.

She stepped out of his embrace. "I'm fine, really. Obviously, Winnie and I have some things to work through. I'm going to give her my bedroom and move my things into yours."

"That's fine. I'll sleep downstairs." He nodded.

"No, that won't do. Winnie knows we're married, Race. How will it look if you sleep somewhere else? She's mourning the loss of her mother. I don't want her to feel like she's displacing you or interrupting marital discord." Millie pinned the last petticoat in place. The dress would need to be washed anyway, so there was no point in hanging it out. She walked toward the back entrance to the shop where the laundry tools were stored.

"Now, wait a minute. We can't share a room."

"Whyever not?" His look of dismay lightened her mood and she tried not to smile.

"Because there's only one bed, that's why."

"True, but it's the bigger bed. You'll just have to not sleep in the middle. Also, you can't be wandering around till all hours of the night. You'll need to be home to help me entertain like a proper husband."

"But…" He worked his mouth like a fish, trying to come up with the words to refute her.

"But nothing. You know I'm right. You can do this one thing for me."

Race hung his head. "Fine. But it doesn't change anything." He looked into her eyes. "I'm sorry about last night, Millie. I was soaked with drink and not myself. I didn't mean to hurt you."

"Race, you only hurt me when you ran off. The rest I quite enjoyed." She placed a hand on his chest.

He stilled then stepped out of her reach. "I'll be upstairs entertaining Winnie. Don't be long." He turned and went up the stairs.

Millie sighed. One step forward, two steps back. She put the dress in the laundry tub and followed Race upstairs.

****

"I'm quite envious of you, Millie. Why, you've been on your own since you were younger than me. With Race, of course, but you worked and lived in different cities and made your own choices about what to wear. I'm tired of living under Father's thumb." Winnie poked at her cornbread with her fork. She used her knife to slice off a chunk then daintily forked it into her mouth.

Shelley White

"It hasn't been all wonderful. I didn't have a mother to guide me." She placed her own bread in her bowl and ladled stew over it.

"But you had Mother's friend, Beth. She wrote to her all the time."

"Bethy is a whore. Did Mother neglect to mention that? She left me to be raised by the man who abused her and a whore." Millie slapped her spoon down on the table. "Don't glamorize my life."

Race, who'd been silent most of the meal, finally spoke. "Winnie, Millie doesn't mean to snap." This earned him a glare from Millie. "Her father forced her to marry me when she was much too young. You've been able to enjoy being a young woman without the responsibilities of a wife."

"But it all worked out splendidly for you." She looked from Race to Millie, who sat in stony silence.

Race's smile looked more like a grimace. "Yes, it's been splendid."

Later that evening, Millie carried a stack of clothing into Race's room and placed it in the wardrobe. Race fluffed the pillows, but it looked more like he was beating them into submission.

"I told her I keep my clothes in that room for convenience sake. I think she owns so many dresses herself, she didn't think to question my needing more space."

Race grunted.

"It's been a full day. I'm going to turn in. Are you coming to bed?" *Be bold*, Millie told herself. She began unbuttoning her dress as she would if she were alone.

Race glared at the bed as if it contained vipers, his head whipped up as he homed in on the movement of

Millie's fingers. "Millie, I…"

She stilled. "Yes, Race?"

He cleared his throat and gave her his back. "Which side of the bed do you prefer?"

"Either is fine. It's your bed. Get in where you feel comfortable, and I'll take what's left."

"Nothing about this is comfortable," he grumbled.

Millie turned to give him privacy as he undressed. She resisted the temptation to sneak a peek. She quickly pulled off her dress and underthings then slipped her cotton lawn nightgown over her head. It was her favorite and it fell to her ankles like a whisper. She heard the ropes creak as Race climbed into bed.

She moved to the table by the door to retrieve her lamp.

"Don't." Race's voice was strained.

"Don't what? Extinguish the lamp?" She turned to face her husband.

"Yes." His eyes were shut tight.

"Don't extinguish the lamp?" What was wrong with him?

"Turn. Off. The lamp. Now."

"That is what I was doing, and you told me not to. What is the matter?"

"Is the lamp out?" His eyes were still shut.

"It is." She felt her way to the bed. She heard Race let out his breath.

"Don't stand in front to the lamp," Race finally clarified.

"How am I to shut it off? You're not speaking sense, Race." She moved to the empty side of the bed and pulled the covers back. She sat and began pulling the pins from her hair. She wouldn't bother with brushing it out since Race was being so testy.

"Mills, when you stood in front of the light, I could see straight through your nightdress."

She set the pins on the nightstand and placed her hands in her lap. "Oh." *Bold, bold, bold.* "Did you like what you saw?"

He groaned. "Get in bed and go to sleep." He rolled to his side. Now that her eyes were adjusting, she could see he faced the wall.

Millie crawled in bed and pulled the covers up around her neck. In her own bed, she tended to sleep in the middle. If that's where she ended up tonight, Race would just have to put up with it.

Chapter 13

Race was in hell. The heat coming from Millie's body only served to make him envision every curve. Because of the poorly placed lamp and her thin nightdress, he didn't have to fill-in the details. Every last one of Millie's lush curves were imprinted on his brain. He'd looked his full for a solid two or three seconds before slamming his eyes shut.

Coupled with the vague images and drunken memories of the night before, Race was pretty sure he was in hell or well on his way. No amount of chanting 'sister, sister, sister' in his head dulled the reaction of his hardened extremity. He prayed she'd fall asleep quickly. If he'd been drunk, as he was the night before, there would have been no saving her virtue tonight. His sobriety only served as a weak, transparent wall between them.

"Race," Millie whispered in the darkness, sending an unwanted thrill up his spine.

"Go to sleep. Please." He heard the rustle of bedclothes as she scooted closer.

"I can't. Please. I hate this between us. I don't understand. You hurt me every time you talk about ending our marriage."

Please don't touch me. "If I stay with you, I'll only hurt you worse."

"But how?"

"I couldn't keep my first family safe." The memory of that failure succeeded in tempering his body's need.

"You couldn't have stopped a disease that killed so many people," she reasoned.

"I lost my mother to the same thing. I should have seen the signs sooner. When our neighbors got sick, I should have packed up my family and moved out of the city. I didn't do enough. I should have died with them."

"If you had, you wouldn't have been there to save me. I'm not a little girl anymore. I understand what would have happened to me. But you've been protecting my innocence for far too long. You have every right to my body, Race, and I want you to have it. I want you. Not as my protector or as my brother. I want a husband. Your actions for the past six years have been nothing but honorable and protective. You have to let go of the guilt you're carrying. I know you want me when you've been drinking. Do you want me now, too?"

Millie's question hung in the darkness between them. Race's member surged to life again. She'd be terrified if she knew how much he wanted her.

"It doesn't matter what I want. I'm so much older than you, Mills. You need someone who's going to be around for the rest of your life, someone who's going to be around to raise your children to adulthood and grow old with you."

"You talk like you're an old man."

"The men in my family don't live much beyond fifty years old, Millie. I will leave you and I will hurt you." He risked rolling to his back. He hated hurting her with his words this way, but she needed to understand. "I had my chance at a family and lost it.

118

Not only do I not deserve a second one, but you don't deserve to be hitched to my sorry wagon. You deserve someone who can offer you a full life."

"You don't know the future. I'd rather take a chance with you for however long fate allows than start over with anyone else. There are no guarantees in life for anyone. I can't be with anyone else as long as I love you." Her fingers grazed his arm. "Think on it Race. If you leave, I'll be the one who's broken. There isn't anyone else for me but you."

There was more rustling as Millie rolled to face the opposite wall. Race stared at the ceiling, thinking on 'it'. Her breath finally evened out in sleep, but still he stared. Could he embrace the second chance right in front of him or should he quit entertaining selfish hope?

****

The next morning Millie went through the motions of opening up the dress shop to the sound of Winnie's incessant chatter. It comforted her, in a way. The girl was too sweet and kind for Millie to be able to hold a grudge, though it was disconcerting how much Winnie knew about her life. While her mother had limited the information she shared with Bethesda about her younger daughter, clearly Bethy didn't use the same discretion.

Winnie asked about her childhood, wedding, travels, and life in Santa Fe. Millie responded vaguely to the personal questions but made up for it by delighting her sister with her impressions of the city and travel experiences.

Though Winnie assured them she'd left a note for her father, Race went to the telegraph office as soon as it opened to send a message confirming Winnie's safe arrival. Millie shuddered at the thought of how far her sister traveled alone. She was fortunate to have arrived safely. Winnie carried on about how brave Millie had been. But she'd had Race at her side. Winnie was the brave one or perhaps simply naïve and foolish.

"All taken care of," Race announced as he came through the shop door. If there's a response, the office will send a messenger.

"Ooh, if there's a response, I don't want to hear it. That's the best part of being far away. Father can't tell me what to do." Winnie made herself comfortable in the shop's sitting area. Her sunny yellow dress poofed around her and she's pulled her hair up into a bun with a braid wrapped around it. The style was far too sophisticated for a place like Wylder, but Millie was impressed her sister accomplished it without the assistance of a ladies' maid.

"Thank you, Race," Millie said.

Race nodded and disappeared into his workshop.

"I like him," Winnie said in a low voice so Race wouldn't overhear.

Millie walked over and sat in one of the other chairs. "Thank you. I'm rather fond of him myself."

"He doesn't boss you around but he's there if you need him. And he's really nice, and handsome." Winnie leaned back in her seat with a dreamy expression on her face. "I want to marry someone like him."

Millie didn't exactly know how to go about sister-to-sister conversation, so she gave it her best shot. "Surely you have beau back in Savannah."

She blew out an exasperated breath. "Yes. John Miller has been courting me, but half the time it feels like he's courting Father. He works at the bank. Father says his prospects are very promising." She picked invisible lint off her dress.

"You don't like him?"

"I don't *know* him. He asked permission to step out with me three months ago. But I've been busy spending time with Mother." She pressed her fingers to her lips as her eyes filled.

Millie waited while her sister composed herself.

"He's come to family dinners and joined me at church. Father is always present and monopolizes the conversation. I know nothing of his hopes and dreams, only of his portfolio and prospects. I don't even know if he wants me for me or because marriage to me would make him heir apparent. How did you know Race wanted you?"

Millie snorted a laugh. "He won me then he paid my father for me."

"What?"

Millie smiled and gave her sister the abridged version of her and Race's non-existent courtship.

"That's so romantic!" Winnie clasped her hands to her chest.

"No, it wasn't. It was chivalrous, I give you that, but romance had nothing to do with it," Millie corrected.

"That may have been so but look how your love grew. You became friends first and you respect each other. You have this shop together. You're truly equal partners. That's more romantic than sweet words and gifts."

Behind Winnie, Race stood in the doorway to his workroom. Their eyes met. Without breaking his gaze, she answered her sister. "Love comes easy when it's your best friend."

He broke away first and backed deeper into his room. Winnie remained oblivious of the byplay between the couple.

"How long do you plan to stay?" Millie refocused on her sister.

Winnie fidgeted in her seat. "I don't know exactly. I wanted to come meet you and get to know you. It's only a matter of time before Father comes for me or sends money for my return."

"I doubt he'll do that. It was very dangerous for you to come all that way alone," Millie scolded.

"Oh, pooh. Don't be a stuffy big sister when we're just getting to know one another. Father will probably come himself when he can get away from the bank or send a maid and one of his lackeys to escort me. I'll probably be here for at least two weeks."

A crash sounded from Race's workroom, followed by a curse and the sound of several things falling on the floor.

"Race, is everything all right?" Millie called.

"Oh, yes," came a terse reply.

"You can stay as long as you like. I'll be more comfortable once we've heard from your father."

"Thank you. I didn't know how I'd feel about meeting you. Mother made you out to be wonderful and elegant, but you're really just a normal person."

Millie took the statement as a compliment since she was sure it was intended that way. "You're not what I expected either. I was prepared not to like you because I felt you took my mother from me."

Winnie reached over and clasped her hand. "Neither of us had a whole mother. I'm sorry that my existence caused her to leave you behind."

Millie squeezed her hand. "Your birth did no such thing. She was unhappy and had valid reasons for leaving. I think she always intended to come back for me. Her failings are neither of our faults."

Winnie smiled. "So, shall we blame my father, then? He wouldn't let her come get you. I love him, but he's very stuffy and concerned about the way things look. I'm sure he didn't want to explain to his friends why my mother came with another man's child in-tow."

"Yes, let's. Then maybe we can both release the hurt and anger we've harbored for her. I am glad you came." They both rose from their chairs and met in a hesitant embrace.

"I may have lost my mother but I'm so happy to have found my sister."

It surprised Millie to discover she was too.

Chapter 14

Race found Millie behind the shop stirring the laundry in a wooden tub. Steam rose, dampening her brow and curling the hairs escaping her bun. He longed to wrap one of the ringlets around his finger. He recalled her nervous habit of pulling the wisping hairs out. The habit faded as her confidence grew.

She looked as tired as he felt. If Winnie's visit was to be prolonged, he would have to come up with an alternate sleeping arrangement for his wife.

Even his subconscious worked against him. He awoke that morning with his arm around her waist and her body pulled tight against him. Already hard, he tried to slip out of bed without waking her. Her sleepy moan almost unmanned him.

Seeing her this way and knowing he caused her misery only reinforced his belief an ill-fated future awaited if they stayed together.

"Who's watching the shop?"

"I put Winnie to work. It's been a slow morning and she can come get me if she needs anything. I showed her how to fill out a repair invoice for your clock customers."

"Thank you. Why are you doing the wash now?"

"I'm taking advantage of Winnie while I can. I'd rather do this now so I can spend the evenings mending instead of vice versa. I know you'd thought to expand the business by adding laundry service, but we truly cannot without hiring someone to help. My hands are already full with making dresses and mending." She wiped away the tendrils sticking to her forehead.

"That was always the intent. I know your skills are better used elsewhere. I need to step out for a bit. I have a friend leaving on the stage shortly and I want to see him before he leaves."

Millie frowned. "I didn't know you made friends here already."

"He's an old friend from Boston. It surprised me to discover he's the Episcopalian preacher who serves this area. He's heading home to care for his mother."

"Did you come across him in your visits to the church?" Her tone was casual, but Race sensed an underlying question.

"I asked Mr. Smithers to send word when the preacher returned to town. I went to see him about an annulment." He placed his hands on the stick to still the agitator.

Millie released it and switched tasks, not meeting his eyes. She lifted a soapy pink dress out of the tub and moved it to one with rinse water. "And is he going to grant it for you?"

"He would not. He said our only recourse is divorce." He watched her hands still.

"Is that what you're going to do?" She stared into the water,

He reached over, tilting her chin so she would meet his eyes. "I don't want to without your agreement. I want you to understand a separation is for the best, but I won't force it upon you. I won't have you carry the burden of that stigma. I would just leave, but then you wouldn't be free to remarry." His stomach churned saying the words, but her happiness outweighed his jealousy. He would have to figure out a way to screen potential beaus from afar.

She jerked her chin from his grasp and plunged her hands back in the water. She violently swished the dress then fed it through the ringer. "Go meet your friend. I won't talk about this now." She picked up the dress and walked over to the clothesline to pin it up.

Race sighed. "Tonight then. We also need to discuss alternative long-term sleeping arrangements if Winnie is going to be staying."

Millie ignored him, so he went back inside to let Winnie know he'd be out.

Race caught up to Preacher Jameson at the livery where he was saying good-bye to his horse.

"I'll walk you to meet the stage." Race clapped his old friend on the back.

"Come back to the rectory with me and I'll let you carry one of my bags." The man smiled at him. "Have you been able to work through your marital problems?"

"No. They're getting worse." Race frowned.

"I've always believed most answers can be found in a pew on Sunday morning." Rocky glanced at Race out of the corner of his eye.

"It's been too long. It wouldn't feel right. After all this time, I don't feel like my faith is there for me."

"Spoken like someone who didn't get what he asked for. The Father won't grant you what you want if it's not what you need. He only wants the best for his children." They were almost to the rectory.

It sounded like Rocky compared notes with Father Donohue. "Spoken like someone who..." Race didn't know what to say. Spoken like someone in tune with God? That was hardly a compelling argument on his own behalf. Instead, he said, "I wish you were going to be around longer. I miss our philosophical discussions."

"As do I, my friend. I have a feeling they would be far more entertaining to me now."

Rocky said good-bye to the Smithers and handed Race a leather satchel. He hefted a second bag up on one broad shoulder and pick up a smaller case. As they neared the livery a sorrowful whinny rang out.

The big man turned to Race. "That's my Magdalene. You'll come visit her for me, won't you? I trust Chet, of course, but make sure she'd faring well."

"Of course."

They turned onto Cheyenne Road and saw a rider approaching from the east. He struggled to control the horse who appeared to be quite done with its inept rider.

"You, there!" he called.

Race and Rocky turned around to see who the man addressed but found they were quite alone.

"This is Wylder, isn't it?" He attempted to dismount. His left foot caught in the stirrup and the horse took the opportunity to sidestep, dragging the man with her. His youth was probably the only thing keeping him from losing his balance. It surely wasn't any sort of skill.

"This is Wylder. Are you looking for someone?" Race asked.

The man freed his foot and smoothed down his dusty coat. He removed his derby, also coated in dust and knocked it against his leg. A plume of dirt transferred itself from the hat to his pantleg, but the man didn't seem to notice.

"I'm looking for Mildred Lowery. I must find her sister, Winnifred, who intended to travel this way." He placed the hat on his head. "I'm John Miller. I should have started with that."

Rocky chuckled.

Race turned to his friend. "Looks like this is for me to deal with. I hope things go well with your mother." He helped Rocky rearrange his belongings so he could claim the bag Race carried. John Miller shuffled his feet impatiently.

"Good luck to you, too, my friend. I hope you get what you need." Rocky continued walking to the stage stop. Dust billowed in the west harkening the coach's arrival.

Race turned to Miller. "Come on, let's go take care of your horse."

"Do you know Mildred Lowery?" He trailed behind Race, who'd taken the reins.

"Yep. She's my wife."

****

"I can't believe Father sent you to fetch me." Winnie crossed her arms and huffed.

"He didn't. I came on my own. When he discovered your note, he enlisted my help to search your room." John Miller blushed like a schoolgirl. "He assumed there must be more than a desire to meet an estranged sister in the primitive west."

"He never wanted Mother to talk to me about her past."

Race watched Winnie soften at the memory.

Miller tugged at his tie. "I, ah, found your collection of dime novels. I feared you'd come here and fall in love with a cowboy before I even had the opportunity to make my case."

Winnie frowned. "You don't make a case when you're courting, John. You take the time to get to know a girl."

"That was my plan, but I wanted to give you time with your mother while she was alive, then give you a period of mourning. You haven't done anything the normal way." He ran a hand through his mussed hair.

"You gave me no indication of your feelings. You spent all your time talking to Father." She huffed and turned from him.

He stepped toward her. "Because it's easier. I can't think of what to say when you're near. You're so beautiful and vibrant and full of life. You make me feel like a dull glass who can only shine in your presence."

"I don't mean to, make you feel dull, that is. I didn't know you felt that way about me."

Race could understand why Miller was a banker instead of a poet. Winnie's dramatics didn't put him off and she seemed to appreciate his awkward attempt at sentiment. They'd probably make a match if he could bring her around.

"From the moment I saw you walk into the bank with your father a year ago, I've thought of nothing but having the chance to make you my wife."

"So, this isn't about your position at the bank?" Winnie finally turned to face John.

"Never! If you want me to quit as soon as we get home, I will. If you want to live here to be near your sister, I'll find a job here." He got down on one knee. "This is not how I planned to do this at all, but I must prove to you the strength of my feelings." John took her hand. "Winnifred Chambers, please say you'll be my wife."

Winnie's face lit up and she clasped John's hands in hers. "You'd really live here?"

"In a heartbeat, as long as it's with you."

Winnie sighed. "Oh, John! Yes, I'll marry you! But don't worry, it's far to dusty here. I'll only make you take me west for visits." The couple embraced.

Millie, who'd been standing next to Race watching the exchange, said to him, "I guess you'd better make the storage room apartment habitable."

Race nodded, glad someone would be getting a happy ending.

Chapter 15

After getting John Miller situated with a makeshift bed and washstand in the future storage room apartment, Millie invited him upstairs to dinner. She and Race gave them privacy that afternoon, to get to know each other while remaining inside the bounds of propriety. By western standards, at least. Now, they made cow eyes at each other over fried chicken and beans.

As she began clearing the table, there was a knock at the door. Goodness knows she wasn't in any mood for more surprise guests. Race answered the door, but he didn't invite anyone in, and she couldn't see past him in the darkness.

"Millie, it's for you," Race said quietly.

"Well, invite them in." Her hands were already immersed in hot dishwater.

"I'd prefer not."

This got her attention. Race was usually polite to a fault. She wiped her hands on a towel and joined Race at the door. Two figures in hooded capes stood on the landing. One raised her head and surprise didn't begin to cover Millie's shock at seeing Adelaide Willowby standing there.

"Perhaps we can talk downstairs in the shop?" Adelaide said.

"Of course." Millie started down.

Race stopped her with a hand on her arm. "What's this about?"

"It's a private matter." Adelaide led the other hooded figure toward the stairs.

"My *wife* does not have private conversations with the town madam; not without me."

Adelaide smirked. "That you know of."

Millie's face heated.

"You may be present, but my business is with Mildred. We'll wait downstairs." The cloaks made the two figures appear to float down the stairs.

Race pulled Millie back to face him. "What did she mean? How do you even know Addie Willowby?"

Millie jerked her arm out of his loose grip. "How do you know her well enough to refer to her so familiarly?"

Race pulled the door shut so their proper guests wouldn't overhear, ensconcing them in shadows. "That's how most around town refer to her. I've never met the woman, but it looks like you have. When?" he growled.

"I went to show her fabrics and patterns. I thought the social club would be a good source of business since there are so few women in town. It was a good idea, too. Mrs. Willowby was happy to receive me." *The first time, at least*, Millie thought wryly. "If you were around more, instead of off walking and hanging around the town's churches, you'd know full well what I do with my time." She jammed her hands on her hips.

"I'm mostly out at night. During the day I was working at Goldmount. I trust you didn't go to that place at night. I think you didn't want me to know of your little visit."

Millie sighed, defeated. "Race, what does it even matter? You want to cut me loose. When that happens, I'll be able to do whatever I damn well please anyway. I'm going to see what *Addie* wants. Join us or not; I don't care." Race followed at her heels as she descended.

He unlocked the shop's back door and ushered everyone inside. Millie lit the lamp. The guests removed their hoods to reveal Addie with her white-blonde hair perfectly coifed in a series of twists and ringlets. Accompanying her was a pale, sickly girl with golden hair piled and pinned haphazardly on her head and enchanting hazel eyes.

Addie started right in. "In case you were unaware, you are one of only two female business owners in the town of Wylder. The other being Eulalia Culpepper." Her nose pinched slightly has she stifled a sneer.

"Race and I own this business together," Millie corrected.

"Not according to the deed on file. This property is in your name alone."

She spun to Race who scowled at Addie. "What?"

He shifted his gaze to Millie. "We'll talk about it later." Then to Addie. "Make your point so we can get on with our evening.

Millie turned, too. "Yes, please. Apparently, my husband and I have a number of things to discuss."

Addie smirked again. "This is Amber. She has found herself in a position not conducive to her current line of work. I heard you were looking for someone to help with laundry service and that you have an apartment to let."

Millie frowned. "None of those things have

happened yet. We've only talked about them. How could you know."

Addie smiled. "The same way I knew about the deed. I have eyes and ears everywhere in this town. I have to in order to protect my girls and my own interests."

"You want us to take in a pregnant—" Race started, but Addie held a single finger up to stop his tirade.

She turned to Millie. "I explained to you why I stay. If I leave, I will have nothing to support my daughter with. I didn't tell you that I've had this discussion with Mr. Willowby as well. If I were to leave, he would make it known to my contacts in the east exactly what business I'm in here. Not only would I have no money and no prospects, but I would be considered a fallen woman and divorcee." Millie flinched and Addie pinned her gaze briefly on Race before continuing. "That said, I decided as long as I must remain here, I will do what good I can. I protect these girls to the best of my ability. Amber is pregnant and Mr. Willowby has barred her from the Social Club. She has nowhere else to go. I am asking you, as a woman who knows what can happen to young girls who don't have anyone looking after their interests, to help me help her."

Millie looked at the bedraggled girl. She'd seen so many like her in Santa Fe. If not for Race, she could have easily ended up like this herself. "What would you have me do."

Addie didn't smile, but Millie sensed she wanted to. "What were to be the terms of the washer woman position?"

Millie glanced at Race, but by putting the shop in her name alone, he'd given her every right to make this decision on her own. "We haven't discussed it yet, nor the plan for the apartment. The only reason it's nearly ready is we have a guest."

Addie tapped a finger to her chin. "Ahh, yes. The beau. Why don't you take Amber on as your washer woman and let her stay in the apartment? Subtract her rent out of whatever she earns doing laundry."

This wasn't a bad solution, though it chafed accepting suggestions from the woman. She looked at Race again. He stood by, fuming, allowing her to conduct business. "For how long?" she asked.

"I will post a letter in the morning to Amber's distant relative. Barring that, she is open to the idea of being a mail order bride in another town, providing the groom is willing to take the child, too."

"That doesn't really answer the question." Millie crossed her arms.

"No. It doesn't. But it saves you having to find a washer woman and it keeps you from having to rent to a man." Addie turned her eyes to Race. "Having a man on the premises might be helpful but could also add to your concerns."

Race nodded and Millie couldn't help but feel she missed something.

"It's up to you, Mills. You could start the laundry service right away," Race said.

Millie looked at Addie. "This does not make us friends. I still think you're awful for abandoning your daughter."

Addie narrowed her eyes. "Of course not. You're too closed-minded to imagine yourself in my or your mother's place. I have enough problems without adding your negativity to my life." She turned and had a whispered conversation with Amber, undoubtedly offering reassurances.

Race had stepped into the apartment and emerged with John Miller's small bag.

Addie directed Amber to the door Race held open for her. She hugged the woman and turned to Millie. "I'll have her things sent over. You'll have a dress ready for me early next week?"

Millie should be grateful the woman asked permission to keep the girl at the shop rather than show up with bags in tow. "Yes. Shall I send it, or will someone come pick it up?"

"I'll send the girl who will be wearing it so she can try it on." She walked to the door and flipped her hood over her hair. "Thank you. Women need to be able to count on one another, despite their differences. The west is too harsh a place not to." She slipped out the door into the night.

Race came and stood next to her. "Now where are we going to put John Miller?"

****

Millie couldn't sleep. If the sounds of John's snoring were any indication, Race wasn't faring any better. Winnie was a sprawler and she slept like the dead. If Millie's poking and shoving didn't wake her, it's unlikely the snoring would either. Winnie and John would make a good match in the respect, at least.

She envied her sister. She would marry a man who loved her enough to chase her across the country. John had been able to follow so close on her heels by taking the stage or renting a horse when train schedules didn't accommodate his haste. He'd arrived saddle-sore and filthy dirty, but no less in love with Winnie. Millie sighed. She couldn't even get the man she'd been married to for six years to admit he loved her. She knew he did. There were many types of love in the world, but none where you lusted after someone you loved as a sister. Race's feelings for her had changed over the years; he just didn't want to acknowledge them.

When they decided that Millie would share a bed with Winnie, and Race and John would bunk together, disappointment flitted across Race's face followed by relief. The previous night had been tortuous for both of them. Millie had intended to press her advantage tonight. She'd given him time to think, unfortunately, now, she'd have to wait to act.

****

As it turned out, their houseguests stayed until Sunday when they were able to catch the train back toward Savannah. Winnie refused to travel by stage and besides wanted to spend more time with her sister and exploring Wylder.

Millie and Race allowed John to escort Winnie around town with warnings about which areas to avoid. Millie wrangled them an invitation to see Rick and Sarah Holt's horse ranch. It was enough for Winnie to realize her dime novel cowboys were much rougher and dirtier in real life, to John's relief.

They received word from Winnie's father, Philip Chambers, to which Winnie responded with the message, GET READY TO HOST WEDDING WITHIN MONTH. FULL STOP. This would surely send the man into a panic, so Race followed it up with an additional telegraph explaining as best he could in as few words as possible. Millie wrote a longer explanation including condolences on the loss of his wife and posted it in the mail.

They waited on the platform as the train appeared to grow larger. Millie held her ground, knowing the massive, smoking, rumbly beast wasn't going to jump the track and run her down. At least not at its approach speed.

Winnie threw her arms around her sister one the last time. Despite what Winnie said about not having her mother's whole heart, she didn't seem to have any trouble trusting it to the older sister she could have resented.

"I'll miss you. You must write me every week and come visit. For all your travels, you've never even seen the ocean. You'll love Georgia. John and I will have a grand house and you can stay with us." The train pulling up drowned out the rest of Winnie's rambling good-bye .

It came to a stop with a loud hiss that made Millie jump. "Race and I will try to make it out that way sometime. I would love to see your ocean." She smiled.

Race helped John see to Winnie's trunks. She was leaving with much more luggage than the small satchel she'd arrived with. Millie worked through three straight nights to hastily sew a wedding dress for her sister. Unable to rest with thoughts of Race in the next room, sewing the dress made good use of her time. She intended to spend the rest of the day catching up on sleep.

Winnie's second trunk was loaded with tanned hides and other rustic odds and ends for the room in her future home dedicated to all things western. She and

John were at the stage of their relationship where he indulged her every whim without question. He didn't know about the bison skull packed in the bottom underneath the hides.

Millie smoothed the blond curls threatening to escape her sister's hair fastener. "Though I'm sorry for the circumstances, I'm glad I got to meet you." She initiated a final hug then released her to John. "Take care of my sister, Mr. Miller. She's impulsive and unpredictable." She smiled at her future brother-in-law.

John smiled as well but it was all for Winnie. "It will be my greatest pleasure." He shook Race's hand and they exchanged good-byes.

The train prepared to leave. Winnie and John took seats so they could wave out the window. Millie returned the gesture. The only family member who ever wanted her was leaving, and despite invitations to visit, she may never see her sister again. She reached to hold Race's hand, thankful when he didn't hesitate or pull away. He was always there when she needed him. She couldn't imagine a life without him.

They stayed until the train pulled away. Race didn't hold her hand the whole way but did put his hand on her lower back. That was nice, too.

****

When Millie next opened her eyes, dusk had fallen. She stretched and yawned, glad to finally have the bed to herself again. The aroma of browned beef wafted into the bedroom. Race must be preparing stew; it was one of his specialties. Millie decided not to dress for dinner and slipped her wrap on over her nightdress.

"Feel better?" Race asked when she padded out of her room.

"Much, thank you. Would you like me to make biscuits?" She joined him in the kitchen.

"I just put them in the oven. You can clean up after dinner." He smiled at her before turning back to the stove.

Millie was done putting off the things that needed to be discussed between them. She pulled her belt tighter and took a fortifying breath.

"Do you still love her?"

Race turned, confused. "What?"

"Do you still love Rosemary?"

"I always will. But I don't think it makes me sad anymore." The corner of his mouth turned up slightly.

"What about Aoife?"

"Who?" Confusion again.

"The Irish papist at the Social Club. The one you've been seeing." She hugged herself, bracing for his answer.

"Mills, I haven't been seeing her like you're suggesting. She's struggling with her faith like I am. I've seen her when I visit the Catholic church. I never felt anything for her other than human kindness and concern. She's a little bristly."

Millie relaxed and took another deep breath. "Rosemary. Do you still yearn for her?"

Race turned back to the stove and slammed down the wooden spoon he still held in his hand. He faced Millie and stalked toward her until he was within arms' reach. "No dammit," he growled. "I only yearn for you. Every day, every hour, for the past two years." He started to reach out, then forced his arm stiffly back to his side.

"Then quit fighting it," she pleaded.

"I'm not what you need."

She stepped into his space and fisted both hands in his shirt. "I wish, for once in my life, someone would let me decide for myself what I need." Her voice rose an octave. "Race, I need you! I want you! No other will do, and I refuse to have anyone else. So, you either choose to be with me or sentence us both to lonely, solitary lives."

****

Race was tired, he'd been tired for a very long time from lugging his burdens around. He wondered what it would feel like to simply give up. So, in that moment, he did. He let go of the guilt he clung to over Rosemary and Mary Catherine's deaths. He let the misplaced shame over his hasty marriage slip away. He released the burden of worry over their age difference.

Millie stood before him, beautiful as ever, tousled from sleep. His *wife*. No trace of brotherly feeling remained other than the friendship between them. She had grown and matured and was no longer the fourteen-year-old girl he married. She was a woman and he wanted her. Oh, how he wanted her.

"I'm sorry, Mills. I'm sorry for not being the man, the husband, you needed me to be." Race covered her hands with his.

"Don't be sorry. Be him now and all is forgiven," she whispered.

He wrapped his arms around her and pressed his lips to hers. He took his time, replacing the memory of their last whiskey-soaked kiss.

Her arms were everywhere at once; pressed against his back, touching his hair, and tunneling underneath his shirt. "Take me to bed, Race. Please, finally, take me to bed."

He scooped her off her feet and started toward the bedroom, still kissing her face and neck.

"Oh! The biscuits!" Millie wriggled to be put down.

Race set her on her feet. "Stay." He pulled the bread from the oven, placed it on the sideboard next to the stew, and moved the kettle off the burner plate before turning back to his wife. She'd removed her wrap and toyed with the buttons down her the front of her gown. He prayed for the stamina to keep up with a woman less than half his age and thanked God for the opportunity.

"Race, I've loved you forever. Make me your wife."

"For the rest of my life, I promise you." He led her to his bedroom and shut the door.

****

Millie followed her husband's movements as he crossed to the window and pulled the mesh shade, blocking most of the setting sun's rays. Her body hummed in anticipation, wanting to dance and scream for joy but it might scare him away. Trying to block the chicken scenario image as it rose unbidden to her mind, she giggled. Race wasn't backed into a corner now; he was a man on a mission.

Race came to her. "What's so funny?"

She laced her arms around his neck and drew him closer as he placed his hands on her waist. "Nothing. I feel...I don't know. Happy, relieved, full. A little nervous."

He leaned in and captured her lips again, kissing her then pulling away. "There's no need to be nervous.

I'll be gentle, I promise. I'll stop if you tell me to."

"Don't you dare stop. We have so much time to make up for." She would die if he didn't continue.

"I love you. I'll spend the rest of my life making it up to you and showing you." He finished undoing the buttons on her gown and slipped it to the edge of her shoulders. "Is this all right?"

Millie wriggled and the garment pooled at her feet, leaving her exposed. His hands skimmed her shoulders and down her arms. One tentative finger trailed between her breasts then caressed the underside of her left one before trailing down her waist and resting on her hip. His other hand cupped the back of her head and pulled her in for a kiss, more demanding than before.

His clothing rubbed against her skin. She unbuttoned his shirt, then slipped off his suspenders. She moved her hands to his waistband.

He lifted her hands and stepped back.

Her eyes grew accustomed to the dim light and hungrily followed his movements as he released her.

Race removed his shirt and tossed it on the chair next to the bed. The suspenders hung loose at his sides. His fingers undid the buttons of his trousers faster than Millie could have managed. He bent to pull off his boots, then slid off his pants and drawers as one.

Millie released the breath she'd been holding. Her husband was magnificent. She traced his beard with her hand, then wove her fingers into the hair on his chest. Her gaze dropped lower where his sex jutted from a thatch of thick dark hair. Not ready to touch it, she stepped closer, so its hot length pressed against her stomach and buried her nose in his chest to inhale the scent she loved.

Race pulled back the bed covers. "Get in." His voice was rough.

She sat on the cool sheets and scooted over to make room. He lay down next to her and she slid down beside him as he pulled the blanket over them. He claimed her lips and kissed a trail to her breasts. She arched to meet him, eager to have him there.

He took her nipple into his mouth and sucked. Millie whimpered and buried her hands in his soft hair. He moved to the other nipple, sucked, and grazed his teeth over the tip. She arched into him again. His hand on her hip stroked her skin, moving ever closer to her center until it caressed the hair between her legs. "Spread your legs for me, Mills."

She complied and his fingers delved deeper, to find her aching, pulsing center.

"You're swollen," Race whispered hoarsely.

"Is that bad?"

"No. Feel this?" He dipped his finger lower and spread wetness over the whole area. "It means you're ready for me. I want to taste you so bad."

"What?" she squeaked. She'd never heard of such a thing. It seemed Bethy left out several details during her hurried wedding day education all those years ago.

His chuckle rumbled against her ribs. "Shhh. Not yet." He continued to spread her moisture, dipping his fingers in and out of her core, deeper each time.

Like before, her body reached for a pinnacle, but she didn't want to go there without Race. The sensation he created was stronger than the last time when they were clothed. She wanted to fall into it, allowing herself to get closer each time it rose. "Race, I need you. Be with me."

He whispered, "Ah, Mills. It might hurt your first time. I want you to enjoy this first."

"No. I want you. Please."

"Don't beg. You make it too easy to give in. It's been seven years for me; I'm afraid I won't have a lot of control."

"It's all right. Bethy told me what to expect. I don't want to wait any longer to be one with you."

In answer, he went back to nibbling her breasts, taking each nipple deep and circling them with his tongue. His finger went deeper as well, pressing and widening her channel. He added a second and used his thumb to stroke her swollen outside.

"Race, now!"

He sat back and held her gaze for a moment before positioning himself between her legs. "Just relax." His fingers spread her open while keeping pressure on her throbbing nub. He guided his length to her opening and rubbed it through her wetness before pressing the tip inside. "Don't hold your breath."

Millie expelled the air she'd been holding. It didn't relieve the tightness she experienced.

Race stilled. His finger concentrated on her nub until the sensations began to rise again and her channel softened. He pressed in without stopping.

She squirmed against the stretching and burning, trying to find a position that relieved one or the other.

"Be still, Mills. It will ease."

And it did, a little. Race began to move. She didn't know how to respond, nothing felt natural. The climax she'd been chasing was a distant memory. Race sped up for three or four strokes before shuddering. He pulled out of her and rolled to his side. He kissed her lips and temple. "I suppose it's a good thing I had a hair trigger. I'm sorry. It will be better next time." He left the bed and padded to the kitchen.

That was it? Millie was bereft. She'd expected, well, not that. The build-up did not at all prepare her for the finish. A tear leaked down her cheek.

Race returned and climbed back into bed. "Here." He pressed a warm, wet cloth to her sore parts. It soothed her.

"Goodnight, Race." She started to turn to her side.

"Goodnight? We're not done. I know it was uncomfortable for you, but I think I can make it better."

"I don't think I can do that again tonight."

"We're not going to do that, but I'm going to make you feel better." He ducked under the covers, his beard brushing her inner thigh. "Open for me."

She spread her legs reluctantly. He moved the warm cloth, exposing her swollen nub. "Race, no. I'm fine. You don't have to do anything."

"Oh, yes. I do. Do you have any idea how long I've dreamed of this? But it will help you feel better, too," came his muffled reply.

His tongue prodded her nub. It both aroused and soothed. He did it again, this time with a long, warm stroke. Heat rushed to the area, causing her sore spots to throb. Somehow, the residual pain intensified the pleasure. As he continued to taste her, pressure began to build until she tipped over the edge and rippling sensations stole her breath and made her spine tingle. It was much more powerful than their first fumbling, clothed attempt.

Race poked his head out from under the blanket. "How do you feel?"

Millie sighed. "Better? I don't really have words. This wasn't what I expected."

"It shouldn't ever be as expected, but I promise next time will be all good." He retrieved the washcloth and went to the kitchen. When he returned, he replaced the rewarmed cloth and pulled her flush against him. "I love you, Mills. We have the rest of our lives to perfect our lovemaking."

She nestled closer and threw her arm over his belly. "I love you. And I have high hopes for this and all other aspects of our marriage. You've been my closest friend for so long, loving each other is the only way to improve upon our relationship."

"Thank you for not giving up on me," Race whispered into her hair.

She placed her hand on his chest over his heartbeat. "I figured I owed you a life-saving. You just needed to trust I knew the best way to go about it."

"Amen to that."

Epilogue

"Race!" Millie squealed as her husband surprised her from behind. He looped his arms around her waist and spun her away from her worktable. "Be careful. I could have been using scissors."

He set her on her feet. "I'm careful. I can't help but watch your every move. I knew you were sorting buttons, but my business couldn't wait."

She pushed the buttons away from the edge of the table. "The business of distracting me from my work?"

He pulled her close and kissed her temple. "No, this business." He pulled a small, hinged box out of his coat pocket.

"A gift for me?" Millie made a grab for it.

Race held it aloft. "Not anymore. You don't appreciate my lovin. I'm gonna give it to baby Estelle instead."

"You'll have to hurry, then. They're moving away soon. Are you planning on leaving me for an even younger woman?" Millie tried to look stern but couldn't hold back a smile.

Millie loved seeing this side of Race, the part that had been stifled for their first six years together. He let the past go and it seemed like a thick blackened scab that surrounded his heart, cracked and fell away. The Race of the past year was lighter and less serious. He'd well made up for the previous years of husbandly neglect.

"Never! What's the blush for? Hmm?" He bent to kiss her neck, mumbling into it, "Where are Amber and the baby?"

Millie giggled as his lips nipped her earlobe. "Gilda, not Amber. It hurts her feelings when you forget. She took Estelle with her to the mercantile to buy soap-making supplies. They'll be back any minute."

Race stepped back with an exaggerated sigh. "You were right, I have a gift for you."

"Whatever for? Our anniversary isn't for another month."

He tapped her on the nose. "Not the anniversary I count. That's today. It's been a year since I came to my senses. It's been a year since I almost gave you up." He pulled her into his arms again. "Thank you for not letting me."

Millie was happier than she'd ever imagined. Only one thing was missing now. "What did you bring me?"

He handed over the box and Millie cracked it open. It contained an oval brooch. The outside was gold filigree with and inner ring of blue enamel and another of seed pearls all surrounding a tiny window. It was lovely.

Millie frowned. "Race, this is a mourning brooch."

He wrinkled his brow. "No, the tinker said it was a keepsake locket." He took it from her and turned it over. "See, you can wear it as a pin or put it on a chain. I spent an hour in the grass to find that tiny four-leaf clover there in the center."

She smiled at his boyish enthusiasm for the gift. "I think the tinker saw an easy mark, but perhaps you're right. I love it, and I love that you put so much effort into making it lucky for me."

"The clover is a place-holder. One day soon, you'll be able to put a curl of our baby's hair in there. I know you've been discouraged, but this is how much I believe it will happen for us." His brown eyes stared deep into her gray ones.

Millie ran her hand through his too-long hair. There were a few more strands of gray at his temples than there were a few months ago. "I want that so much, I do. But if it doesn't happen, I'll be content to just have you. I love you so much, Race."

"I love you, too, Mills. Don't be discouraged. Believe."

"I'll wear this always. And I do believe. I do and have always believed in us." Millie kissed her husband with the promise of a bright future, built on the foundation of respect, friendship, and love.

A word from the author…

Reading is my ultimate escape. I love light, feel-good romances in most genres and heat levels. This is my first foray into historical fiction and writing spicy bits. All my books can be found listed on my webpage.

www.shelleywhitewrites.com

https://www.facebook.com/shelleywhiteauthor/

https://www.goodreads.com/author/show/21635067.Shelley_White

https://www.amazon.com/Shelley-White/e/B099FNKT5X/ref=ntt_dp_epwbk_0

Thank you for purchasing
this publication of The Wild Rose Press, Inc.

For questions or more information
contact us at
info@thewildrosepress.com.

The Wild Rose Press, Inc.
www.thewildrosepress.com

www.ingramcontent.com/pod-product-compliance
Lightning Source LLC
Chambersburg PA
CBHW071944170626
46813CB00005B/1824